THUNDERING HOOVES

Brandon gave a yell of warning, bringing up his rifle at the same time. Lambert stumbled sideways, tripped and fell. With an angry snort the buffalo thundered down on them. Brandon fired, placing a bullet from his high-power rifle clean between the animal's eyes. The great beast paused and staggered, mortally wounded. But it had already done its worst.

Poor Lambert, right in the path of its forward rush, was swept from the ground and carried forward to the very edge of the drop into the pit. He cried out in alarm and fear.

The buffalo dropped stone dead in its tracks.

Brandon darted forward, trying to stop Lambert from falling ...

REX BRANDON
JUNGLE HUNTER

JUNGLE ALLIES

by

DENIS HUGHES

Published through
arrangement with
Cosmos Literary Agency

The *Rex Brandon: Jungle Hunter* stories are works of their time. Occasionally, certain outdated ethnic characterizations or slang appear, which contemporary readers may find objectionable. To preserve the integrity of the author's words, these obsolete aspects have remained in place for this edition. The text is presented as it originally appeared.

Editor: Philip Harbottle, Cosmos Literary Agency

Book and cover design: Rich Harvey, Bold Venture Press

Bold Venture Press, August 2023.
Available in paperback and electronic editions.
Published through arrangement with Cosmos Literary Agency.

Copyright © 1951 Denis Hughes.

Copyright © 2019, 2023 the Estate of Denis Hughes.

REX BRANDON: JUNGLE HUNTER TM & © 2023 The Estate of Denis Hughes. Used with permission.

Originally published in the United Kingdom by Curtis Warren.

This is a work of fiction. Though some characters and locales may have their basis in history, the events and characters depicted herein are fictitious.

No part of this book may be reproduced without written permission from Cosmos Literary Agency or the publisher.

JUNGLE ALLIES

1

"No White Man Lives..."

THE jungle seemed to spread out in every direction, extending like some sprawling green monster with a pulsing life of its own. No breath of wind penetrated to the gloom of its innermost depths; yet there was no silence or stillness. The constant chatter of monkeys made the air hideous. Mingled with the din, as if using the raucous noise for a background, millions of birds of every shape and colour flew erratically from branch to branch, singing and chirping incessantly. Small creatures scurried this way and that, darting swiftly over tangled roots or freezing into immobility whenever danger seemed imminent.

The age-long life of the vast Congo jungle continued unchanged.

Steaming under the torrid glare of the tropical sun, the uppermost leaves of the dense tree growth covered a world of twilight, almost unlimited in area, a world in which the law of self-preservation reigned supreme.

It was through this great basin of river-intersected forest land that a small party of human beings were making their way. Owing to the density of the jungle, and the innumerable dangers that beset the path, their progress was necessarily slow and laborious, but always the party was gradually advancing south and west towards the coast.

Heading the long line of burden-carrying native bearers was a solitary white man. Sweat was pouring down his face as he hacked and slashed a way through the matted lianas that hung in festoons from the trees all round. He wore soiled white bush garb, and his sun helmet was thrust to the back of his head as he forced a way through for the bearers to follow. Every now and again he would stop, listening perhaps, or taking a quick check with his compass to ensure that he was not wandering off his general line of advance.

Walking close behind him, wielding a broad-bladed machete, came a tall, loose-limbed native. Unlike the rest of the party, he was not burdened with cases of stores, but carried two high-velocity rifles slung from his shoulders.

The white man paused, tipping his helmet a little further to the back of his head as he wiped the sweat from his brow and grinned good-naturedly at his near companion.

"Getting near the big water now, N'gambi," he said. "I'll not be sorry to leave this hell of green stuff for a while."

N'gambi showed his big white teeth in a broad grin. He was devoted to his employer, and had been with Rex Brandon ever since Brandon had hired him as headman for the native bearers of a previous expedition. It had not been the Belgian Congo on that occasion into which they had penetrated, but Brandon had been so struck by N'gambi's faithfulness and ability as a tracker that he had persuaded him to come along with him when he made the present safari.

As a world-famous geologist and big-game hunter, Rex Brandon had many calls on his services, and now he was returning from a highly successful expedition into the deepest parts of the great Congo Basin. The Belgian Government, in collaboration with other Western powers, had employed him to survey certain mineral resources which were reputed to lie concealed along the upper reaches of the Congo and its many tributaries. Now he was on his way back to civilisation, bringing samples and detailed reports of his findings.

It had been a long and arduous trip, but results would prove it to have been well worthwhile in the eyes of the geological world. Brandon himself was satisfied at having done a job and done it well.

"I, too, shall be glad," said N'gambi, "for this country is not my own and its dangers are many. There are strange tales of the things that lie hidden in the jungle."

"We've seen a few of 'em ourselves," answered Brandon a little grimly as he started forward again after a glance behind at the string of fifteen natives who plodded along with a patience found only among the races of the mighty African continent.

When the safari began Brandon had had nineteen bearers, but various accidents had reduced that number. He had been fortunate in not losing more men; and fortunate, too, in the fact that N'gambi had succeeded in keeping them loyal to him under the trying conditions with which they had met.

On several occasions Brandon's incredible swiftness of action and first-class marksmanship with a rifle had saved them all from far more serious losses.

Here in the depths of the jungle there was no night and day, but a sort of twilight shot with green and a blackness when the sun went down that was absolutely impenetrable, so thickly did the foliage grow above the heads of the little party.

"Come on," said Brandon firmly. "I'm hoping to reach the Chuapa River by sundown. We'll make camp there for the night."

N'gambi nodded wisely. The Chuapa was one of the smaller tributaries of the Congo, feeding down to the main river. When they eventually arrived at the Congo itself they would complete the rest of the trip by boat, which might or might not be a less hazardous undertaking.

Headed by Brandon and N'gambi, the party continued after a brief rest.

Some hours later Brandon sniffed the air and turned his head to N'gambi. There was a faint smile on his lips as he did so.

"Smell water?" he inquired.

"Yes, *bwana*. Much water ahead now. I smell crocs, too. That is not so good; but it may not be bad. We cross the Chuapa?"

Brandon strode on, slicing through the fronds of big tree ferns and tangled lianas as he went. The heat in this place was terrific, yet there was little light.

"Yes," he said presently. "We'll cross; but not till morning. I don't fancy a river crossing in darkness."

"That is well, *bwana*," answered N'gambi with a nod.

A faint lightening in the semi-gloom told them that somewhere ahead the trees were breaking and thinning. At the same time the stench of river mud and rotting vegetation reached their noses strongly. Myriads of mosquitoes pinged and hummed around them, making life more unpleasant than it had been before.

Then the trees and undergrowth grew perceptibly less dense. Brandon could see for several yards ahead now. A few minutes later they sighted the Chuapa, a wide, shallow stream of sluggish water running between steaming mud-banks that appeared to be nearly a mile wide on either side.

N'gambi touched his employer's arm and pointed. Brandon, following his gaze, shaded his eyes against the sudden glare of the afternoon sun. Free to reach down now, its rays were intensely hot and blinding as they sparkled and shimmered on the stretches of stinking mud.

Halting and staring ahead, Brandon saw the ugly shapes of basking crocodiles, as the creatures lay and sunned themselves on the fringes of the river bank.

"Peaceful enough at the moment," muttered Brandon. "I wouldn't give a lot for the chances of a man if he fell among them though." He smiled tightly, his handsome tanned face creased up as he reached out for one of the rifles N'gambi carried. The man handed it over in silence.

"Tell the men we rest here tonight," said Brandon. "I'm going downstream a bit to see if I can bag some food for the pot."

N'gambi nodded wordlessly, then watched as Brandon set off quietly in the direction of the river flow.

Brandon was tired after the strenuous day, but he felt that if he allowed himself to rest immediately he would not feel much like going after a few river birds once he had settled down. Better to go straightaway he told himself.

He did not have to go far from the point at which the party had struck the Chuapa before he sighted a flock of small African duck. They were considerably larger than their European counterpart, and one would make a useful meal. He set himself to approach the feeding birds with as much caution as he was capable of. The rifle he carried was of small calibre, used chiefly for light game. It was not really a suitable weapon for killing duck, but Brandon was such an expert shot that he knew he would be able to kill a bird without damaging the body.

What he had not thought about when he set off was the fact that a small calibre weapon would be useless against anything of a dangerous nature.

He was still several hundred yards from the peacefully feeding ducks when his sharp eyesight lit on something that completely distracted his attention from the birds.

Sudden movement out on the shimmering mud brought his head round and his rifle up instantly. The movement was that of one of the enormous crocodiles, raising itself on its short legs and making with a surprising turn of speed for the fringe of undergrowth that edged the mud.

Brandon knew well enough that such a move could only have been dictated by the fact that something in the way of food had suddenly shown itself.

He began hurrying towards the spot for which the croc was making.

Breaking his way through low-growing marsh vegetation, he saw the cause of the saurian's sudden interest.

It was a sight that brought his heart to his mouth for an instant, for he realised in that moment that he was armed with too light a rifle to deal with the crocodile.

Staggering blindly down towards the mud-bank of the river was a dishevelled figure. Ragged bush garb hung limply from his spare frame, and his head was bare. He moved as if blind from exhaustion, walking with a sort of dreadful mechanical gait that was now carrying him straight towards the swiftly-approaching crocodile.

Brandon had to act quickly. He doubted if his rifle would penetrate the scaly hide of the hideous croc, but unless he did something quickly the lone white man would walk straight into the creature's gaping jaws.

Dropping to one knee, he brought his rifle up and aimed at the crocodile's left eye. The creature was a good hundred yards distant, closer to the exhausted man than Brandon.

The sudden crack of the light rifle caused the man to halt in his tracks, swaying and peering about in a bemused fashion. The glare of the sun struck upwards, blinding him so that he saw neither the crocodile nor Brandon.

The crocodile, its eye pierced by Brandon's bullet, turned and thrashed about on the half-dry mud, mad with pain and fury. Brandon was running fast now, knowing that unless he reached the lost man in time he would blunder even closer to death. But the crocodile, a monster of its kind, soon recovered from the shock of Brandon's long-range bullet. It turned its attention to the lone man again, beginning to advance on him once more.

Brandon was shouting to the stumbling figure now. Suddenly the man saw his danger and tried to run, but only fell to the ground after a few steps. He tried to rise, but failed. Brandon paused for long enough to put another bullet in the croc, which slowed it down. Then he was close to the fallen man. He reached the man's side almost at the same time as the crocodile.

Firing again, straight into the creature's gaping jaws, Brandon grabbed the man by the shoulder and started to drag him back out of harm's way. But the croc was tough. It came on again.

Brandon paused, looking this way and that. There was nothing for it but to deal with the monster as best he could. He allowed it to come close to him, then, as its vicious, teeth-edged mouth came open, he forced the barrel straight down the reeking throat. With a snap the jaws were shut, tearing the rifle from his grasp in a moment. But Brandon just had time to pull the trigger before he lost his grip.

The croc gave a convulsive heave.

Then Brandon was getting the fallen white man clear of the threshing creature's vicinity.

Once off the mud flats that fringed the river, he lowered his burden to the ground in the shade of some scrub and examined the man. He was not quite unconscious, but not far off it. Brandon saw him as a young man, dirty and tattered, but with a pleasant face underneath the lines of strain and fatigue that etched his features.

Brandon un-stoppered his flask and forced some of the raw spirit between his swollen lips. The young man's eyes opened vacantly.

"Chizma..." he whispered. "Chizma... No white man lives ..."

Brandon grinned reassuringly. "Sounds quite a yarn," he said. "Come on, back to my camp."

2

Sole Survivor

N'GAMBI, after giving orders for the making of camp, heard Brandon shooting. He also heard his shouts when Brandon was trying to warn the lone white man, and, though he knew nothing of the adventure his employer had had, he set off at once to find out the reason for the unusual noises.

It was N'gambi, therefore, who arrived just when Brandon needed assistance most. Between them they got the stranger back to camp, where he was made as comfortable as possible. The treatment brought quick results, so that before the sun had set that evening Rex Brandon was listening to as strange a story as he had heard in many years.

Once the young man he had rescued was more like his usual self, there was no stopping him from telling his yarn, and as it progressed Brandon soon understood the urgency that drove his latest visitor.

"I'm Jeff Lambert," he told Brandon. "You won't have heard of me, of course, because I'm only a technician really, but you may have heard of Professor Cochran. Walt C. Cochran they call him over in the States." He raised his eyebrows inquiringly as he glanced up at his rescuer.

Brandon frowned for a moment. Then: "Good heavens, Lambert! You mean the American anthropologist? Yes, of course I've heard of him! In fact I've met him on one occasion. Is anything wrong with him? When did you see him last?"

Lambert smiled weakly. Then he shook his head in grim silence before answering.

"I'm sorry, Brandon," he murmured. "Cochran is lost to the world. But there are worse things than that ... Can you spare a cigarette?"

Brandon nodded quickly. A pipe-smoker himself, he sometimes used a cigarette, so was always supplied with them for emergencies such as this. He said nothing to Lambert beyond giving an encouraging grin when the young man had lit up and sucked in a lungful of smoke.

"I was the photographic expert with Cochran," said Lambert a moment later. "I don't know if you remember, but he was trying to locate something that would explain certain traces of ancient civilisation in the deepest part of the Congo Basin."

Brandon nodded sagaciously. "I did hear something about the proposed expedition," he admitted. "But it started quite a while ago, didn't it?"

"Nearly a year," answered Lambert quietly. "All went well enough till just over four months ago. The Professor was getting along like a house on fire with his own obscure investigations when we struck disaster in chunks that were much too big to cope with." He paused. "Before I go any further," he went on, "I think you should know that there was a girl in the party." His mouth tightened as he said it. "She's a prisoner of some strange tribe at the moment—or was when I last set eyes on her." He broke off and looked up at Brandon.

Brandon gave a puzzled frown, meeting the young man's gaze in a worried fashion.

"How bad was it?" he demanded tensely. Lambert drew on his cigarette again, dropping his eyes from Brandon's face.

"Pretty much a wipe-out, I'm afraid," he said slowly.

"Tell me about it!" Brandon's voice was suddenly-edged with hardness. It was not aimed against Lambert, but was caused more by the thought of a lone woman in the hands of some tribe of hostile natives than any other consideration.

"I'm coming to it," answered Lambert. "Still feel a bit hazy about it all myself, so you'll have to forgive me if I don't sound too lucid." He gave a faint smile.

"Take it easy," Brandon told him, relaxing himself.

"There were five whites in the safari," Lambert said. "Cochran, myself, the girl and a couple of other fellows who were with us for the hell of it in the hope of getting some big-game shooting. They're both dead now, so they don't matter a lot. Names of Jenkins and Hausmann." He broke off, collecting his somewhat scattered thoughts.

Brandon said: "Who was the girl?"

Lambert looked up. "Naomi Jensen," he replied. "She's a journalist covering the expedition. I hope she isn't dead; she was a good sort."

"Go on," murmured Brandon.

Lambert frowned a little. "Cochran didn't have a lot to base his search on," he said. "He'd been looking into something else up in Nigeria when he picked up a few clues that set him thinking. Someone came on a dying man in the jungles of the Congo and passed on the yarn to Walt C. as a matter of interest. The Professor lapped it up like a kid and was all raring to go, but it took a little time to organise the business. That was when Naomi and I appeared on the scene.

"According to the story Cochran heard this dying man had mumbled a few words before passing out. They, and a bit of a rough map, were all that Cochran had to go on. The dying man had said: 'Chizma... people of the Sun...no white man lives to tell.' Then there was something garbled about gorillas being on guard.

"Cochran secured the map—which was not a very detailed one, incidentally—and started to organise his safari when he reached the Congo. There was no snag as far as the Belgian Government was concerned and everything started smoothly. We got well out into the interior and started to follow the instructions of the map Cochran had. This dying white man wallah had seen ancient ruins, it seems. They were marked, but not much else. It was the bit about the People of the Sun that had tickled the Professor's curiosity and prompted him to make the trip."

Lambert paused and studied the ash on the end of his cigarette.

Brandon watched him for a moment, then brought out his pipe and stuffed the bowl with care, his long, brown fingers working in an unhurried manner which in itself was a lesson in patience.

Lambert continued: "Then we ran into trouble when we were only a few miles from the site of these rumoured ruins and the stretch of country around them."

"What happened?" put in Brandon quietly.

"Some crazy native bridge collapsed," said Lambert wryly. "We lost a good half of the bearers, as well as nearly all our stores and ammunition. It was just at the end of the rainy season then, and the river was swollen: into a torrent, as well as being alive with crocs." He hesitated and gave a shudder at the memory. Then:

"Walt C. was magnificent! He had the rest of the party reorganised in next to no time, but it wasn't to be. No sooner had we started off again, with a much smaller; group this time, of course, than we struck it really bad."

"How so?" Brandon's eyebrows were raised slightly.

"Elephant stampede." answered Lambert in a clipped tone. "The brutes caught us unawares and simply flattened the entire outfit! I've never experienced anything so horrible in my life—and I've seen some things, believe me! The herd just trampled those poor damned natives underfoot, to say nothing of Jenkins and Hausmann, poor devils.

"It was only by the grace of God that Cochran, Naomi and myself escaped. We happened to be outside camp at the time, stalking a forest buck or two, when it happened. You can guess how we all felt when we dashed back and found what the din was about!"

"Yes, I can well imagine it," admitted Brandon. He realised that Jeff Lambert, though young, was a pretty tough man, but his past experiences had told on him to a certain extent. His nerves were jagged now, and it would be some time before he would once more be a thoroughly steady person.

"But," said Brandon slowly, "surely the elephants didn't wipe out *all* the bearers? Some of them must have got away."

"Four escaped," answered Lambert. "The Professor was right on top of the situation again, turning up trumps when the business seemed at its worst. But there must have been a jinx on that expedition. It was never destined to meet with success in my opinion. The words of the dying white in the jungle sort of made it worse. '*No white man lives to talk,*' or something of the kind."

Brandon grinned humourlessly, his lips tightened up. "You're going off track," he scolded gently. "Keep off superstition, Jeff! It never did pay dividends, my lad. What happened after the elephants?"

"Sudden attack by the wildest savages imaginable," said Lambert tersely. "Poor old Walt C. Cochran went down with a spear sticking in his hide; I was knocked for six by a throwing club; and I'm sorry to say the Naomi Jensen was carried off by our attackers. I just caught a glimpse of her being grabbed before I was hit myself.

"When I came to everything was quiet. The four of our party who'd survived the elephant stampede were lying about, dead. There was no sign of the Professor's body, though, so I guessed the savages must have taken it off with them. I suppose they'd have carted me away as well only I happened to have fallen sideways into some thick bush and been hidden." He paused unhappily, staring in front of him with unseeing eyes. "What worried me more than anything else, though, was the capture of Naomi.

"I found I could still walk all right, so after a bit of rest I started off to follow the natives. I might even have found the girl if I hadn't got lost in the jungle; but there it was. I did get lost, good and proper as they say!"

Brandon nodded understandingly. "It's not a difficult thing to do in this country," he said. "You wouldn't be the first white man who's walked a hundred yards from his camp and never returned." He paused. Then: "And I take it you've been wandering around ever since?"

Lambert nodded. "I was just about at the end of my tether when you picked me up," he replied. "Lucky for me that you happened along when you did. I've never said thank you properly yet, but you know how feel about it, Brandon. I'll always remember what you did for me."

"Forget it," said Brandon tersely. "You and I have a lot more important things to do besides talking."

Lambert got up from the canvas safari chair on which he was sitting. His fists were clenched tightly as he looked at Brandon. There was a light of excitement shining in his eyes as he gained an inkling of what the tall geologist had in mind.

"You mean you're going after Naomi?" he said. "By God, Brandon, I'd do anything to save that girl! If I hadn't been lost like that I might at least have found out where the swine carried her off to; but as it was I'm as much in the dark as you are. There must be *something* we can do!"

"There is!" replied Brandon with a grin. "First of all you're going to get some proper rest; then we'll have another talk and get the details straight before we decide what steps to take to rescue this girlfriend of yours!" He grinned broadly and slapped Lambert lightly on the shoulder.

Lambert flushed a little under his tan. He was a good-looking boy, thought Brandon. And he must have plenty of guts as well to have survived the hardships of a lone trek through the mighty Congo jungle. Brandon felt he wanted to help him; wanted to help the unfortunate girl I too, but a lot would depend on the boy himself.

"I can't rest!" objected Lambert. "I'm perfectly fit now, thanks to you. Can't we discuss this business now? It must be weeks and weeks since Cochran's safari came to grief. I lost track of time completely, so I can't say for certain how long ago it was; but Naomi's in terrible danger! You've got to realise that."

Brandon smiled. "Keep your hair on, son," he advised. "If she's still alive now she'll stay alive till we find her. I don't want to damp your spirits, Jeff, but the odds are against these savages showing much mercy to anyone—even a woman. In any event a day or two longer won't alter the position. You've got to rest up—till tomorrow at the earliest; then we'll decide what to do."

Lambert's lips were compressed as Brandon's words sank in on his mind. "I don't care what you say," he burst out. "I'm still positive in my own mind that Naomi is alive and well. But she's a prisoner, and we've got to get her out as quickly as we can!"

"We will!" Brandon assured him. "But you can't rush a thing like this. Have you got that map you mentioned?"

Lambert thrust a hand inside his tattered bush shirt. He brought out a soiled piece of paper and smoothed out the creases as he spread the map on the little table in the tent where he and Brandon had been talking.

"Here it is!" he said excitedly, pointing with his finger. "It's only luck that I had the map at the time of the attack. Cochran had been showing it to me; I was actually holding it in my hands when the natives attacked us. Somehow or other I kept it. It was automatic, I suppose."

"People of the Sun," mused Brandon as if he hadn't been listening. "What does Chizma mean, Lambert? Do you know?"

The younger man shot him a glance. Then: "As far as I gathered from Cochran it's probably the name of this ruined city the old boy was hunting for," he replied. "But why do you ask?"

"Nothing...." Brandon strolled to the tent fly and bent to look out. Dusk had fallen and the air was alive with insects. "Get some sleep," he said to Lambert. "I'll make up my mind for sure, but I think we'll look for Naomi!"

3

Rogue Tusker!

Brandon, when he left Lambert inside the tent, walked across to where N'gambi and the rest of the bearers were squatting round a fire, cooking the meal. They greeted him with cheerful grins, for though the journey had been a dangerous one there was something about Rex Brandon which men of every race and creed were bound to admire and respect. It was a quality that had stood him in good stead on more than one sticky occasion in the past — and would probably do so again in the future.

"N'gambi," said Brandon, "I would talk with you. Come."

The headman rose to his full height and followed his employer silently as Brandon strolled off to the edge of the circle of firelight.

"You are troubled by the stories of the white man, *bwana?*" he murmured when Brandon had been silent for a moment.

"Perhaps," admitted Brandon. "N'gambi, have you ever listened to tales of a lost city or a race or a strange people called Chizma? People of the Sun ..."

"*Bwana,* there are many such tales in this land. Most of them are lies told by faithless men to gain money and wives from unsuspecting seekers. Does this white man try to fool you with such a story?"

Brandon laughed bleakly. "No," he said firmly. "He does not try to fool me, N'gambi. And he does not lie. If he does, it is I who am a fool, and I don't think I am." He broke off, staring into the thick bush that fringed the banks of the broad sluggish river. Then: "I asked you because you are wise and know things that white men cannot know. But if Chizma means nothing to you then perhaps you are right."

N'gambi bridled slightly. *"Bwana,"* he said quickly, "I do not say that. I said only that there are many such tales. Now I will tell you. I have heard among my own people—many moons' travel from this place—that a strange people dwell in the jungles of the Congo. It is said by the wise men that these people have the burning Sun for their god. That is all I can tell you. If the *bwana* wishes to search for their place of dwelling I will go with him, but the tales are bad about these people."

Brandon nodded. "Thanks for the warning," he said. "It is not yet decided what will happen, but I think I shall go in search of them." He turned and met the native's eyes. "If the other white man speaks the truth these people have captured a woman. There may yet be time to save her life, N'gambi. Now return to your fellows, but speak not of what I have said. Silence is a better thing till our minds are made up, you understand?"

N'gambi nodded once, then turned on his heel and went back to the camp-fire.

Brandon remained aloof for a short time, thinking and checking up in his mind on various points. He already knew in his heart of hearts that on the morrow he would turn back and seek to locate the ruined place from which he thought Cochran's party had been attacked. But he still liked to think it over before plunging himself into an adventure which had nothing to do with his life-work as a geologist, though it would not be the first time he had done such a thing.

Though the night was never entirely quiet a measure of peace settled over the little camp on the banks of the River Chuapa. Darting night creatures set up their own special scurrying sound; occasionally the scream of something caught by something else reached the ears of the men in their sleep. The sullen splashing of crocodiles was audible out in the slow-moving stream of water; the faintly distant cry of night birds made music against a background of scuttling sounds. In the very far distance of the forest depths some larger animal roared defiance to the moon that was blocked from its view by the close-growing foliage and tangled, matted lianas.

Night was fast over the great Congo country.

For more than an hour after returning to his tent, Rex Brandon churned things over and over in his mind. He had already decided quite irrevocably to follow up the trail that the coming of Jeff Lambert had given him. Now it was just a matter of making up his mind as to the best ways and means of carrying out his determination to do all in his power to rescue the hapless Naomi Jensen. He was a little on the doubtful side as to whether the girl was still alive or not, but if there was the slightest chance that she was he knew it was his duty—as well as his inclination—to see what he could do about it. Also, of course, Lambert's story in its entirety had fired his adventurous soul to boiling point. There could be no turning back or avoiding the issue that lay ahead.

In the end he dropped off into an easy slumber that remained undisturbed till the first flush of dawn was stealing over the sky in the East.

Undoing his mosquito net and pulling on his clothes, Brandon went outside the tent, to find that Lambert was already up and ready to move—whichever way Brandon dictated.

"Well?" he said eagerly, as the two of them were standing watching the bearers preparing the morning meal.

"Well?" echoed Brandon with a faint smile which nevertheless carried a hint of reassurance.

"You're not going to let those savages get away with it, are you?" demanded Lambert feelingly.

Brandon shrugged. "That, my lad, is something out of our control," he said slowly. "But don't get all steamed up, Jeff. If Naomi is still in the land of the living, and we can find her we darned well will! That's what I have to say on the subject! Now we can get down to cases." He broke off as N'gambi approached.

"*Bwana,* in an hour the men will be ready to move," said the tall, raw-boned native, glancing obliquely at Lambert.

"Good!" answered Brandon. "I have thought during the night, N'gambi. All is arranged in my mind. The party will follow a different route from now on."

N'gambi's face did not alter its expression of respectful blankness.

"It is well, *bwana,*" he replied smoothly. "Where you lead I will bring the others."

Brandon nodded. "Tell them," he said, "that there will be much money extra for their services when we finally return. Have them ready as soon as you can, and send us our breakfast as quickly as possible."

N'gambi nodded silently, turning on his heel with the hint of a smile at the corners of his wide mouth.

"Efficient fellow, that," murmured Lambert.

"Yes," agreed Brandon. "We're quite old friends as a matter of fact. There isn't much N'gambi wouldn't do for me."

"You're a lucky man to gain such respect," said Lambert.

They sauntered back to the tent where one of the bearers was already setting out their breakfast on a small camp table.

"Give me that map you showed me last night," said Brandon quietly. "If I remember aright it begins at a stretch of country approximately a hundred miles from where we are at the moment, doesn't it?"

"Something like that," answered Lambert. He felt in the pocket of his bush shirt and brought out the map, handing it to Brandon without a word.

Brandon spread it out and studied it closely. There was only one place name marked on it, and the whole thing was so crudely devised as to be little more than a rough sketch. However, he had little difficulty in identifying more than one landmark that was marked on the sheet of paper.

"If this is anywhere near accurate," he said presently, "we ought to be able to locate this mysterious place and see what's happened to Naomi. We leave in an hour."

"You'd better keep the map, in that case," said Lambert. "I'm still entirely lost as to where I am, and you haven't told me, so I wouldn't be much use as a guide!" He gave a rueful grin.

By late afternoon that day they had burrowed their way back into the green hell of the dense Congo jungle and were not very far from a spot which N'gambi informed them was the site of a pygmy village.

"We might learn something there," grunted Brandon. "At any rate we can spend the night with the chief and see what he has to tell us about things in general." He glanced at Lambert. "Always useful to get all the information you can about any particular territory," he added for the young man's benefit. "One never knows what these natives can tell you, and unless you play along with them for a bit, and accept their hospitality, they're apt to go completely dumb on you—even if there's a lion sitting right at your shoulder."

Lambert laughed, but Brandon's words had had an effect on him. He realised that Brandon knew what he was talking about—if no one else in the world did.

"I'm entirely in your hands," he said. "But I do hope we can save Naomi. That's really all that worries me."

"Understandable enough," grunted Brandon.

They pressed on as swiftly as they could through the densely matted jungle, coming at last to a small clearing in the trees where they sighted a large number of rude mud huts thatched with big leaves.

Brandon was on the point of walking straight into the village when he stopped abruptly, motioning his followers to slow down their advance.

"Something funny about it," he murmured to Lambert.

It was true enough. A great majority of the little huts were flattened as if something tremendous had stormed through the village and created havoc.

Brandon turned to N'gambi behind him and raised his eyebrows.

"*Bwana,* something comes here," N'gambi said.

Brandon hid a smile. "That's pretty clear," he said, "Elephant, I should say. A big one at that."

"Looks as if it scared all the natives away, whatever it was," put in Lambert. "There isn't a living soul to be seen."

"They'll turn up presently," answered Brandon. "Come along; we might as well make ourselves at home."

Sure enough they were hardly inside the limits of the village before a small black naked figure appeared on the far side of the clearing and hurried towards them.

It proved to be the chief of the pygmy tribe, and when he saw Brandon and the guns carried by N'gambi he was all smiles.

After a little discussion with the chief Brandon turned and explained the situation to his companions:

"There's a rogue elephant terrorising the neighbourhood," he said. "An old male turned spiteful on account of being wounded during the last hunt these people had. Usually they manage to kill even elephants with their poison darts, but I take it this one proved a little too tough for them!"

"What are you going to do?" queried Lambert.

"Kill it for them," Brandon replied without hesitation. "That is if I get a shot at the brute!" he added. He turned to N'gambi. "Bring salt and present the chief with a bag of it," he ordered. "Tell him to bring his people back to the village and prepare them for a big elephant hunt. It is told!"

N'gambi issued orders to that effect, while Brandon went on talking with the pygmy chief. Presently the gift of salt was brought, handed over with much smiling and nodding of heads, after which Brandon and the chief settled the arrangements for an early start in the morning with some of the best pygmy trackers in the tribe. Everything was planned to the last detail, and when at length the safari turned in for the night Brandon was confident of success on the morrow.

Only Lambert looked askance at the plan, for he considered any such thing as an elephant hunt after a cunning old rogue would be a gross waste of time when the life of Naomi Jensen was perhaps even then at stake.

But Brandon was adamant; besides which it was his safari. He was also under the impression that good would come of it if he succeeded in ridding the village of the terror that had crushed and flattened most of their houses.

With Lambert, N'gambi and the pygmy trackers, they set off a while before dawn. The going was difficult, but the path taken by the tusker was not a hard one to follow. By noon one of the diminutive pygmy hunters reported to Brandon that the tusker was close in front. There were certain signs which, to the practised eye of the tracker, were quite unmistakable. Brandon, too, was in agreement with the little man.

Advancing cautiously, they continued on their way.

A small clearing in the jungle revealed a stagnant pool of water. On the muddy bank of this there were marks of the enormous feet of the elephant. To Brandon's amazement the marks were still wet with water where the great beast had ploughed through the mud and come out on the other side. The tusker was indeed close!

But hardly had he voiced his opinion very quietly to N'gambi and Lambert before they were startled by a sudden squealing roar and the crashing of branches not fifty yards distant.

An instant later the vast bulk of one of the largest male elephants Brandon had ever seen in his life was bearing down on them with the speed of an express train. Its large sail-like ears flapping, trunk held high and white tusks gleaming in the dim light, the creature thundered down on them.

Brandon knew there was not a moment to lose. Like a flash he dropped to one knee, bringing up the heavy elephant rifle to his shoulder as he did so. The natives gave wild yells of dismay, scattering in every direction. Then Rex Brandon squeezed the trigger of his rifle and sent a .55 bullet crashing into the frontal bone of the elephant's skull.

The creature pitched forward on its knees, almost turning completely over. But a moment later it was struggling to its feet again, to make one last desperate attempt on the life of the white man who had come to kill it.

Brandon pumped a second shot into its right eye. This stopped it again, and, as it proved, it never rose.

But it only stopped its forward rush when it was less than ten yards from the spot on which Brandon himself and his companions had been gathered when the attack was made.

Brandon had not moved an inch; Lambert, although armed only with a light rifle, had stood his ground; while N'gambi, stout-hearted as he undoubtedly was, had run for cover. Of the remainder of the little hunting party there was nothing to be seen.

However, immediately they saw that the mighty creature was dead the pygmy trackers reappeared and joined the white man they now considered to be their saviour.

When Brandon and his friends returned to the village there was a tremendous welcome waiting for them. Brandon did not understand how word had reached the chief that the tusker was dead, for the pygmy trackers had remained with him, but there was a feast already prepared when they reached the village.

The celebration continued long into the night, and when at last Brandon thought it was time they got some much-needed sleep the chief, who could not do enough for them, accompanied Brandon and Lambert to a hut that had been set aside as a guest house for the visitors. Brandon would have preferred to occupy his own more hygienic tent, but for the sake of not hurting the little fellow's feelings he had reluctantly agreed to such hospitality.

It was, however, a complete surprise when the chief, after seeing them safely inside the hut allotted to them, made a great show of bringing something from a fold in his skimpy loin cloth and presenting it to Brandon with the utmost gravity. Brandon, thinking it to be some native *ju-ju,* accepted it with equally grave mien. But when he examined the present the chief had given him he caught his breath in his throat, for never had he seen such a priceless gem.

Lambert, too, was temporarily speechless at what he saw.

Brandon held in the palm of his hand an enormous diamond set in exquisitely worked yellow metal that could only be gold. The diamond caught the weak light of an oil lamp and turned it to brilliant fire. Brandon whistled, turning to the chief. He wondered where on earth the primitive pygmy had obtained such a stone, but it required all his skill and tact to elicit the information.

When at last he had worked the pygmy chief into a mood in which he would talk freely he learned that a white man had once come to the village many moons ago. The white man had been sorely wounded and almost dead when he arrived. He had subsequently died in the village, although nursed by the women of the tribe. But before he died he talked a lot in delirium—the chief did not put it quite like that, but it was plain what had happened—and spoken many times of something called Chizma and the people of the sun.

Brandon said nothing of the thoughts that were running through his head, but a great excitement was welling up inside him.

When the chief finally left them to find what rest they could he and Lambert eyed each other. Then Brandon looked down at the precious stone that rested in his hand.

"Chizma," he murmured thoughtfully. "Jeff, do you realise that this stone must have come from the place we're looking for? From the place that Walt C. Cochran was looking for? And probably from the same place where your girlfriend is being held a prisoner?"

Lambert nodded wordlessly, swallowing in his throat.

"Incredible, isn't it?" said Brandon.

"I can hardly believe it!" burst out Lambert.

"I think it's true enough," answered Brandon slowly. He grinned. "Worth an elephant hunt, wasn't it?"

4

CRY OF TORMENT!

BRANDON and his safari bid farewell to the pygmy village and its friendly little inhabitants as dawn was breaking next morning. The people would have liked them to remain as their guests for considerably longer, but the urgency that had prompted them to penetrate the jungle fastness made them restless, so that although Brandon himself would have liked to stay a little longer he thrust the idea out of his head. The life of a white woman might rest on their speed.

Before they set off he had another talk with the chief, learning, among other things, that the dying white man who had brought the jewel to the village had come from the east, a region of dense jungle and many dangers. It was, said the chief, an unwise thing for anyone to enter that district.

Brandon thanked him gravely, promised that on their return they would pay another visit to the village, then gave him a hunting knife as a token of his friendship before going out at the head of the safari.

The days passed uneventfully, piling up into almost a month before they were anywhere near the district which they thought would be their ultimate goal.

It was not until then that they struck any further sign of human beings. And when they did find it they were not impressed by friendliness, but almost open hostility. Coming on a broad river unexpectedly, they saw groups of natives on the muddy shores. These people caught sight of them at about the same time, but unlike most other tribes they did not show any interest or alacrity in greeting the unusual visitors to their district. Instead they slipped away with furtive glances, disappearing into the bush with barely a sound. Brandon looked at Lambert and grinned.

"Seems they don't like the look of us," he commented. "I suppose they have a village somewhere nearby; we'd better find it and see what we can learn. If my reckoning and your map are anything to go by we must be getting fairly near the source of that jewel and the end of your own trip."

Lambert only grunted in response.

They carried on, skirting the shores of the river and making in the general direction taken by the natives when they sloped off.

Following a narrow jungle path which was obviously used frequently, Brandon suddenly halted at sight of a group of unfriendly looking natives who barred their path. They were tall and well-built. But this was not the best time to study them from an anthropological point of view.

The savages were armed with spears, which they poised as if ready to throw at a moment's notice.

Brandon raised his arm in the universal sign of peace, advancing slowly as he did so.

The group of natives stood their ground till he was only a few yards from them, then they backed away, though still in a threatening manner.

He tried several dialects on them, but none seemed to be understood, so that in the end he shrugged and turned to re-join his companions. Lambert was watching curiously, ready to shout a warning if Brandon's back was in danger. The bearers, though respecting Brandon deeply, were plainly nervous. Even N'gambi seemed to sense that there might be trouble brewing in the near future unless Brandon handled things very carefully.

"No good," said Brandon tersely. "Either they don't understand my language or they don't want to! We might as well press on, ignoring them. They seem to be a pretty wild sort of outfit." He glanced over his shoulder, to see the natives still standing in a group with their spears at the ready.

"Our way lies across the river, *bwana,*" murmured N'gambi. "I think perhaps that these unfriendly people imagine you are come to steal their hunting and their wives and their crops. It would be well if we continued on our way."

Brandon smiled faintly, then nodded to Lambert. "Have the men build a raft," he said to N'gambi. "We will cross the water towards the rising sun."

Under the watchful eyes of the group of natives the scene of business began. Trees were cut, hacked clean and lashed together by strong ropes of twisted lianas. The party spent the whole of that day working on the project. At night they built fires and settled down around them, keeping a close watch on all sides, for Brandon was by no means sure of the temper of the hostile savages. He knew quite well that everything they did was being watched from under cover, though now there was no visible sign of the watchers.

With dawn they were once again hard at it. Brandon and Lambert refrained from going out with guns to find game, for they thought it wise not to show off their ability to kill with the strange weapons they carried. Also, of course, they were influenced by a desire to remain close to their men in case the savages tried any tricks.

By mid-day on the following day N'gambi reported that everything was ready for the crossing of the river. Brandon, who had watched the construction of the big raft with expert eyes, gave a nod. Then he surveyed the surface of the river over which they must pass.

It was fairly wide, but not over-deep, though too deep to be forded, hence the building of the raft. He and Lambert selected the point at which the crossing should be made. The raft itself had been built on the edge of the water; now it was heaved and levered out and away from the bank into the shallows. Sweating men laboured with long poles as they moved the raft to the place indicated by Brandon. There, it was loaded with cases of stores and equipment, including Brandon's precious mineral samples from the first part of his jungle journey.

They were ready to cross. The raft was large and capable of carrying the entire party. Brandon, though normally a cautious man, would have liked to have taken the whole lot over in one journey. He decided, however, that it would be wise not to do so in case of accidents. N'gambi, therefore, was ordered to divide the bearers into two lots, sending the first batch across with the stores and cases.

And then it was that trouble descended on them swiftly.

Without a word of warning a large and war-like party of the hostile natives emerged from the undergrowth and came towards them at a run, brandishing clubs, spears, and bows and arrows. The air was suddenly thick with flying arrows, while long-shafted spears whistled down on them from the high angle at which they had been thrown.

Brandon whirled round, seizing a rifle and raising it. Several of his party were struck and brought down by arrows or spears. Then the rest were yelling their heads off and leaping onto the already moving raft. For long minutes there was nothing but pandemonium on all sides. Brandon and Lambert were firing on the savages with deadly effect, but they were seriously outnumbered. In the end it seemed only sensible to retreat while they still had the chance.

There was nowhere to retreat to but the river and the raft, now several yards out from the sloping mud banks of the shore.

"The river!" yelled Brandon tersely. "Make for the raft, Jeff!"

Lambert emptied his magazine into the attacking savages, bringing down a couple of them and wounding three more. Then he and Brandon glanced round, saw that they were the only members of the party still on shore—apart from the dead—and ran hell for leather down the mud bank to the water.

Splashing through the shallows amid a veritable hail of arrows, they finally gained the raft. N'gambi had stayed on the shore until the last minute, making for the raft just as Brandon ordered the retreat. Now he was squatting on the clumsy log structure pouring out bullets from his rifle as covering fire. Meanwhile the rest of the party were poling the raft further out into the stream with frantic energy. Being unarmed themselves, they did not have the courage of their companions; besides which they had seen several of their fellows go down beneath the spears and arrows of the attackers.

Brandon heaved himself onto the raft and lay panting for a second while Lambert joined him. Then they were reloading their rifles again and shooting across the strip of water at the whirling figures of the fanatical natives.

A wail of anger went up from the enemy as they saw the safari party slipping through their fingers, but Brandon's fire disheartened them and before long they slid out of view among the close-growing scrub and thorn bushes of the shore.

Brandon lowered his rifle and looked at Lambert.

Lambert had been unlucky enough to receive a slight wound from a spear blade in the first onslaught. N'gambi was tending it now, while the remainder of the bearers were making good time with the clumsy raft.

"Queer turn-out, wasn't it?" said Lambert grimly. "What the devil did they start on us like that for, I'd like to know?"

Brandon shrugged. "Couldn't say for sure," he replied. "Might have been the look of us; more likely the last safari that passed this way treated them badly or something of the kind and they didn't intend to stand for any nonsense with us."

"Hmmm... Could be you're right," grunted, Lambert. "Anyhow, I'm glad we got out of it more or less in one piece."

"We lost six of our men," Brandon pointed out.

The raft was now in mid-stream. Occasionally Brandon caught sight of crocodiles wallowing in the water, or lying immobile with only their flared nostrils showing above the surface. On the shore they had recently left he had a fleeting glimpse of more than one dark figure slinking about through the scrub.

He turned his attention to the far bank. It was very similar in character to the one they had left, but sloped upwards more steeply, with a belt of thick foliage and baobab trees coming almost down to the water's edge.

It was while he and Lambert were studying the bank for a suitable landfall that one of the pole-pushing bearers gave a wild cry of alarm and dropped his pole, darting back to the centre of the raft. Brandon swung round, following the man's terrified gaze. A babble of voices broke out among the others. The raft drifted downstream at an angle. Then Brandon saw what had caused the commotion. He grabbed a heavy rifle and dropped to one knee on the gently swaying platform of the raft.

Bearing down on the raft with a snorting noise was the massive bulk of a giant hippopotamus.

It must have surfaced quite close to the raft, for there had been no sign of it a moment before, unless it had been floating with only its nose showing, so still and silent that its bulk had passed unnoticed. However, it was now less than ten yards from the raft, and moving quickly through the water.

Brandon squeezed the trigger of his rifle. All would have been well had not fear among the bearers driven them to seek the far side of the raft. The vessel gave a lurch which upset Brandon's aim just sufficiently to spoil his shot.

He cursed as the hippo disappeared below the surface, then realised an instant too late what was likely to happen.

Shouting to the others to hang on, he felt the raft lifted beneath him. It cocked up at an alarming angle, the cases of stores and mineral samples broke loose from their ties and slithered over, making the list even worse. Then the diving hippo came up again and struck the vessel once more, tipping it right up on its side so that the yelling bunch of natives were shot off into the water, together with the stores and cases. Brandon found himself floundering about in the thick muddy water. He still held his rifle, but all round him was a scene he would remember for a long time to come.

None of the bearers could swim. Some were clinging to the upturned raft, but a large number of them had been carried downstream by the slow-moving current. In a moment or two the crocodiles would finish them off. The thought of the crocodiles made Brandon use his eyes more keenly than ever. He saw Lambert swimming for the bank with a powerful stroke, glancing over his shoulder every now and again. Then he sighted the woolly head of N'gambi in the water a yard or two from him. N'gambi, he knew, was not a swimmer. Striking out rapidly, he reached the headman, grasping him firmly and starting to swim for the shore.

N'gambi, frightened though he was, had the sense to keep still, and was even able to take the rifle from Brandon while he did the swimming.

Hardly had they started for the shore together when the first scream of terror heralded the attack of crocodiles on the helpless bearers. There was nothing Brandon could do about it, and the realisation turned his heart sick within him as he thought of his faithful men being killed and eaten by the razor-toothed saurian monsters of the river.

Swimming fast, and taking N'gambi with him, he finally reached the bank and stumbled ashore. By this time Jeff Lambert was already on dry land, firing as fast as he could at the crocodiles that were wreaking such havoc among the unfortunate men in the water. Brandon and N'gambi quickly joined him, but they knew it was a hopeless battle. There were far more crocs in the river than they could ever shoot, and the scent of blood, fresh-spilt, brought many more on the scene. Under the eyes of the white men and N'gambi every one of the surviving men were lost, dragged down by the ever-hungry jaws of the crocodiles.

At last Brandon lowered his smoking rifle and looked across at Lambert.

"That's that," he said grimly. "We're in a hole and no mistake this time! It looks as if we've lost everything. My samples, the stores, ammunition and the men!"

Lambert grunted miserably. He visualised the end of their search and rescue attempt.

But N'gambi had somewhat better news. Standing on the bank close to the water, he gazed downstream, hand raised to shield his eyes from the glare of the sun on the glistening water. When he turned there was a faint grin on his face.

"*Bwana,*" he said, "we do not lose all as you think."

Brandon gave a start, then hurried to where his headman was standing. N'gambi pointed downstream. Strung across the water about a mile further down was a low bar of sandbanks, broken here and there by channels.

"Much of the stores and boxes will be stranded there," said N'gambi. "We do not have men, but we still have our guns and there will be ammunition and food saved as well."

Brandon nodded. He remembered that one or two of the ammunition cases had been more securely fastened to the raft than the majority of the gear. The raft would undoubtedly drift downstream to the sand bar, to be stranded there. If their luck was changing they would be able to retrieve some of the lost equipment.

"Come on," he said quietly, striking off along the bank.

On the far side a group of savages who were primarily the cause of the disaster were dancing about jubilantly, for the whole dreadful thing had happened before their furtive gaze.

At the sand-bar the party found as many supplies as they could carry. Ammunition had been Brandon's chief worry, but this was relieved at once when they saw that several cases had been carried down with the raft, which arrived at the bar about the same time as they did.

Loaded up with stuff, they made their way to the bank again, to rest a while and discuss the situation. It was not a very good one, but Brandon was determined to make the most of it.

"Now we've got this far we might as well carry on," he said. "It'll mean a lot more hard work, of course, but according to our reckoning we can't be very far from the place where Cochran came to grief. We're in the general area anyway, though it's hard to locate a spot exactly in this sort of country."

Lambert brightened up considerably at his words. He had imagined that Brandon would veto carrying on with the bid to rescue Naomi, but he did not know Brandon for the man he was.

N'gambi, when the idea was put to him, was as ready as anyone to fall in with Brandon's lead.

By late afternoon the three of them were once again on the move. Walking by day and camping at night, they continued to penetrate the jungle for another week's march, by which time Brandon felt sure that they must be somewhere close to the mysterious place known as Chizma.

Tired and weary, they finally reached another native village, only to be met by an atmosphere of nervous tension among the primitive people who inhabited it. Though they were not attacked, it was plain that they were not welcome. Brandon tried to gain information, but met with little success.

Dark eyes flashed warningly when Brandon mentioned the name of Chizma, but he could get nothing beyond a stare for his trouble.

The natives were evasive, offering no hospitality, so Brandon decided to carry on without delay.

"Did you get this far?" he inquired of Lambert. "With Cochran, I mean?"

Lambert shrugged. "I think we must have approached from a different direction," he said. "I certainly don't recognise anything around here."

"What was the situation of this ruined place supposed to be like?"

Again Lambert could not tell him.

It was noon on the following day when they found the woman, staked out on the ground in spread-eagle fashion.

The pitiful cry of torment that reached their ears led them to her.

5

Gateway to Terror

At the time when they heard the cry Brandon, Lambert and N'gambi were plodding along a narrow, winding jungle path. There seemed no end to the density of green around them, and they almost wished they could catch a glimpse of the sun, however hot and scorching it might be. Down here in the green gloom of the forest the heat was sticky, moisture being sucked upwards in a constant thin steam.

Brandon paused as the faint sound reached his ears. He glanced across his shoulder at Lambert behind him. Then the thin, high-pitched cry was repeated.

"What on earth's that?" queried Lambert irritably. The sweat and the flies were jagging his nerves by this time.

"It isn't an animal," answered Brandon curtly. "Come on, let's find out what it is! Over in that direction somewhere." He raised his hand and pointed away to the right of the jungle path.

Lambert grunted, but his interest was aroused for all that. The three of them slung their rifles and hacked a way through the wilderness with keen-bladed machetes.

A hundred yards of laborious going brought them to a steep slope running down with unexpected suddenness. They paused involuntarily, looking about in some bewilderment. Then the cry that had brought them off their original course was repeated, much louder and even more pitifully this time.

"It came from down there!" said Lambert excitedly. Before Brandon could counsel caution the younger man was almost running down the slope, breaking his way through the low scrub that clothed the hillside. Brandon himself wasted little time in following, though he did so with more care than Lambert. He was puzzled by the slope, for he had not imagined that the Congo jungles contained very much in the way of undulating ground, being mostly swamp and flat forest country intersected by meandering rivers and streams.

Brandon could not get any real idea of the lie of the terrain owing to the density of the foliage, but he was under the impression that they were descending into a sort of big basin, choked with forest growth. Even viewed from the air it would not show up as anything but a slight depression, for the trees merged in completely with the surrounding mass.

Then Lambert halted abruptly, cursing softly as he stared ahead.

Brandon, halting beside him, caught a glimpse of grey stonework through the tangle of branches and leaves.

"Ruins!" gasped Lambert in an awed whisper. "Do you think we've actually stumbled on Chizma, Rex?"

"It could be," murmured Brandon. He was listening intently as he spoke. Very faintly there came the sound of a whimpering cry, more like a sob of despair than anything else.

"Beyond the stonework!" he snapped. "Come on!"

They hurried forward, with N'gambi, startled-looking, close on their heels.

Scaling the low remains of an ancient wall was simple, but beyond it was nothing but more and even thicker scrub. They forced a path through it, tearing their clothes and scratching their flesh as they went.

After perhaps twenty yards of this going they broke out into a small clearing; and here it was that they found the woman.

There was something horrible in the sight of her lying there, stark naked, on the ground with her wrists and ankles tied securely to short wooden stakes buried in the earth. With arms and legs stretched wide she was utterly helpless, her glistening black skin completely exposed to the burning rays of the sun as it beat down through the break in the trees.

Arranged in a circle around her were a number of plates of food and gourds of water, but they were obviously there for purely ceremonial purposes. This, thought Brandon, was a grim sacrifice of some sort.

Nor was the plight of the woman ended with her hideous position.

Lambert suddenly gripped Brandon's arm and pointed.

"My God!" he said. "White ants! They're making for the poor wretch in hordes!"

Brandon saw the long stream of tiny white insects as they began to wend their way across the clearing towards the staked-out victim.

In a moment he and Lambert were running forward. It was a race against the ants, but the white men won by a small margin. Even as the first of the vicious little creatures were beginning to crawl over the sweating black body of the woman, he and Lambert were slashing the strong cords through and dragging her to her feet.

Between them they carried her back to the shelter of the rained wall, lowering her gently to the ground. How long she had been where they found her they did not know, but she certainly could not stand on her own feet, but lay limp and slack where they put her, eyes closed now and breathing quickly.

"She's only a girl!" exclaimed Lambert.

Brandon grunted and nodded. "Some tribal business, I expect," he said. "I hope no one was watching us or we shall be in trouble pretty soon!" While he talked he was looking the black girl over. He put her age at about sixteen or seventeen. She was well-developed and pretty. Beyond the fact that she was suffering from a bad fright there seemed little wrong with her physically; she certainly carried no wounds or marks on her body that either of the men could see.

Brandon gave her a drink from his brandy flask, followed by a draft from N'gambi's water canteen. She opened her eyes and stared at them in wonderment.

Brandon tried what he thought might be a local dialect on her and was somewhat surprised to find that she understood it without difficulty. Speaking slowly and in a low voice he began to question the girl. Her name, they discovered, was Tsakim, and by slow degrees they learned her story.

"This is the land of the People of the Sun," she told them nervously. "I shall die and it was not right that you save me from death as you did, but I am glad."

"Why were you left to die?"

"At the full of every moon my people must sacrifice a maiden from our village to appease the spirits of the Sun god who dwell in this place," she explained patiently. "It was my turn, and I was brought here for the purpose, to be blessed and left as a sacrifice."

"Wait a minute," put in Lambert; "do you mean that you come from the People of the Sun?" He frowned.

She shook her woolly head. "The People of the Sun, who dwell in Chizma within these walls, are bad," she said. "My own people are afraid of them, for it is they who order the sacrifice at the full of the moon."

"I see…" murmured Brandon thoughtfully.

"What are these Chizmans like?" inquired Lambert. He sat back on his heels in front of the girl, watching her with narrowed eyes.

"They are a terrible people," answered Tsaldm simply. "They are neither black nor white, and their hair is long and straight. Few men have seen them. No one who enters their place of dwelling returns alive, but I have heard many stories."

Brandon scratched his head a little doubtfully. He knew he was faced with something of a problem.

"I think we ought to take you back to your village, Tsakim," he said at last.

Her eyes widened in fear. She sat up straight and grasped his arm in a pleading manner. "If you do that," she said, "the witchdoctors will have me killed at once for escaping the sacrificial death. It will be terrible dishonour for me! I would rather die here than return to my people! You cannot take me back!"

Brandon frowned. He glanced at Lambert and N'gambi, sitting patiently a few yards away. "In that case," he said, "there's only one thing to do. You'll have to stay with us and take your chance."

"The great *bwana* means it?" whispered the girl. A slow smile touched her mouth. "I will be your slave for ever!"

Brandon grinned. "I don't want a slave," he said. "But you can help us a lot." He paused. "You see, Tsakim, we are seeking a white girl who we believe to be a prisoner of the People of the Sun. We will not take you into danger if it can be helped; but we shall not leave you here to die or take you back to your home. If you are to die, it is already written; the manner of death does not matter, but I do not think you will die for a very long time."

Tsakim blinked at him; then her mouth dropped open in fear as his words sank in on her mind. She gulped. Then she rose to her feet, swaying a little, and drew herself up to her full height. There was something infinitely proud in the way in which she held herself; like a small and beautifully made black goddess, thought Brandon.

"My life is yours," she said quietly. :"Wherever you go I will follow. If fear makes me hesitate you must beat me."

Brandon smiled at her reassuringly. "You won't get a lot of beating," he replied. "And now we must be on the move, for time passes quickly. Are you strong enough?"

She nodded firmly. Brandon jerked his head to N'gambi.

"You will look after Tsakim," he said.

N'gambi showed his big white teeth in a happy grin.

"*Bwana,* it will be simple." He looked at the girl, who eyed him fearlessly. "N'gambi has no woman of his own," he added thoughtfully. "This one is good; I can tell it, even if she is not of my own tribe, which is far away."

Brandon and Lambert exchanged a glance, then smiled at each other. Things ought to work out well, decided Brandon.

With somewhat vague instructions from Tsakim, they set off once more through the jungle, this time penetrating more deeply into the hollow where they had rescued the girl.

Occasionally they came on scattered piles of ruined masonry which spoke mutely of some ancient city that had once stood in the hollow. Tsakim informed them that a day's march would bring them to the Well of Chizma. Brandon was puzzled by the term she used, but did not question her more at the time.

They slept that night in a silent thicket of trees that completely hid them. During all the time they had been moving through the hollow they had not seen or heard any sign of a living man or woman, though game was plentiful enough.

Next day they continued, till Tsakim told them they were close to the edge of the Well.

"Why does she call it a well?" asked Lambert blankly.

"Maybe that's what it is," grunted Brandon. "We'll soon see!"

Some distance farther on they could hear the sound of falling water. It was a noise which caused the two men to look at each other wonderingly for a moment.

"Waterfall?" queried Brandon. "I haven't seen any signs of a river in these parts."

Tsakim said that there was a waterfall, but she herself had never penetrated this far and had therefore not seen it.

Brandon grunted, the sweat pouring down from beneath his sun helmet. Loaded down with stores as they were, the going was harder than it would otherwise have been.

Then they halted, startled and surprised by what lay in front.

Dropping away almost sheer, was what might be called a great pit. From where they stood on the edge of the drop it seemed to be nearly a mile in diameter, though it was difficult to tell exactly owing to the dense foliage that covered the sides. At least a hundred feet below them lay a green tangle of trees and scrub, with here and there clearings in it. Stonework and masonry were glimpsed in the clearings, but the attention of the explorers was caught by something that was revealed on the far side of the well. Clustered right under the lee of the steep wall of the pit were dwellings, but whether or not they were used it was impossible to say at that distance. From any other angle they would have been invisible, for the side of the well appeared to have a considerable overhang at that point.

Tsakim was openly scared as they looked out across the Well of Chizma.

"So that's Chizma, is it," mused Brandon quietly. "We should take a little more care, I think. It wouldn't be clever to get ourselves caught before we begin!" As he spoke he backed into the cover of the undergrowth, still being able to look down into a large area of the great well.

"Do you know a way down, Tsakim?" he asked of the girl.

She nodded fearfully. "There is only one way down," she replied. "The sides, men say, are too steep to climb, though I do not believe it myself. But somewhere there are steps cut from stone which lead to the bottom of the well."

"Then we'd better find them," grunted Lambert.

"Aren't they likely to be guarded?" objected Brandon mildly. "Personally I favour a direct descent—after dark of course. We may well learn something useful by staying where we are and watching for signs of life."

"I was forgetting the rumours about the gorilla guards," admitted Lambert ruefully. "But I can't believe them myself,"

"There are many things the white man does not believe," put in N'gambi quietly. "All things are possible, *bwana.*"

Lambert raised his eyebrows, but said nothing more. There seemed nothing he could say in the face of N'gambi's succinct remark.

They found a suitable place to conceal themselves and spent some hours watching before anything of interest showed itself. Then they had their first clear sight of a Chizman.

This event was heralded by various sounds and movements that riveted their attention for some considerable time.

Brandon was almost growing bored with the way thing were going when they were startled by the clear notes of a silver-toned hunting horn drifting up from the bottom of the well. The horn was like nothing any of them had ever heard in Africa before.

This unexpected sound was followed shortly afterwards by the appearance of a group of shambling figures that crossed one of the clearings below. With something of a shock Brandon identified them as shaggy haired gorillas, but what amazed him even more was the fact that they moved in ragged formation as if marching.

"So they weren't just native rumours!" exclaimed Lambert. "I wouldn't have believed it if I hadn't seen it with my own eyes!"

"Wait a bit," warned Brandon in a slightly worried tone of voice "Do you realise that those creatures are making for the wall of the well close to where we are? It wouldn't surprise me at all if they aren't guards out on patrol."

Lambert sucked his breath in noisily. "By heaven!" he said. "I believe you're right, Rex!" He broke off, straining his eyes as he peered down through the foliage at the floor of the pit. Then he suddenly stiffened and gripped Brandon's arm tightly. "Look!" he gasped. "They aren't alone! There's a man walking behind them! This is the most incredible thing I've ever come across."

Brandon said nothing, but stared hard at the spot that Lambert indicated. He saw that there was indeed a man moving in the rear of the marching animals. It was a tall, copper-skinned savage of some kind. But, unlike the men of the African jungles he was accustomed to, this one was wearing a brief sort of kilt that looked as if it was made of chain mail as it swung and reflected the sunlight dully. His chest, too, was covered in similar material, but his head was bare, the hair being long and straight, reaching to his shoulders.

The hidden watchers stared in wonderment at what they saw. Brandon realised that here was a lost race if ever there was one, and the thought brought excitement among his other feelings.

The strange man and his gorilla charges disappeared as they left the clearing and were swallowed by the jungle again.

"Well, we are seeing life!" grunted Lambert. "Look, Rex, what about moving along and trying to find these steps? If those people ever leave their pit we'd be better off if we knew where they made the exit."

Brandon digested the suggestion for a moment, then nodded agreement.

He and Lambert set off cautiously, leaving N'gambi and the girl where they were with orders to remain in hiding till they returned.

Brandon and his companion had covered a good half mile before they came on anything of interest. Then it was not a flight of steps that halted them, but the growing sound of tumbling water.

"That must be the waterfall we heard a while ago," said Brandon.

They advanced further, coming to the edge of a deep sided gully down which a torrent of water was flowing swiftly, to vanish in a lace of spray over the edge of the well.

They halted and peered around curiously, following the course of the water with their eyes.

Then two things happened almost simultaneously.

The silver notes of the distant horn rang through the air, this time with some subtle hint of command in them.

Brandon glanced obliquely at Lambert, cocking his head on one side as he did so. Lambert grunted, then turned his head sharply back to stare at the thick bush at their backs. As he did so there was a tremendous crashing sound in the undergrowth. Almost before Brandon had time to swing round the terrifying shape of a great water buffalo charged into view, straight for Lambert and himself.

Brandon gave a yell of warning, bringing up his rifle at the same time. Lambert stumbled sideways, tripped and fell. With an angry snort the buffalo thundered down on them. Brandon fired, placing a bullet from his high-power rifle clean between the animal's eyes. The great beast paused and staggered, mortally wounded. But it had already done its worst.

Poor Lambert, right in the path of its forward rush, was swept from the ground and carried forward to the very edge of the drop into the pit. He cried out in alarm and fear.

The buffalo dropped stone dead in its tracks.

Brandon darted forward, trying to stop Lambert from falling; but he was already too late. With a horrible choking cry the young photographic expert clawed at the edge of the drop. His fingers tore out clumps of coarse grass as he grabbed to save himself. The grass roots gave and let him down before Brandon could gain a hold on him.

Brandon, stunned by the suddenness of the tragedy, lay flat on his face and strained his neck in an effort to see Lambert's body. But there was no sign of it. The trees grew thickly below, and by the time Lambert's body hit the ground it would have been completely hidden.

Cursing viciously to himself, Brandon stood upright, a sensation of disaster running through him as he thought of the loss of Lambert. The man had been a good friend, and as well as that Brandon had grown to think very highly of him since their unusual meeting on the banks of Chuapa River.

6

The Death Cage

Sick at heart, Rex Brandon made his slow and unhappy way back to the place where he had left N'gambi and Tsakim. It was no consolation to him that he had just killed the finest specimen of buffalo that had ever crossed his sights. He was glad the beast was dead, but his feelings were more in the nature of revenge than anything else.

N'gambi, who had heard the sound of the shot that killed the buffalo, came to meet his employer. Brandon being alone caused the tall headman to pause in his tracks, and the look on Brandon's face told him that something was wrong long before his employer spoke.

"The *Bwana* Lambert is no more," said Brandon grimly. "He was thrown over the edge of the pit by a buffalo."

N'gambi dropped his gaze in sorrow, for he, too, had grown to like young Lambert a great deal. Nothing more was said between them, the N'gambi thinking it better to leave Brandon in peace for a while.

He returned and passed on the tragic news to Tsakim, who, though she barely knew her companions, was duly sympathetic. But oddly enough her sympathy was directed more at N'gambi than anyone else. The young native girl had already found a certain affinity between herself and Brandon's bearer.

Brandon, who used his eyes as much as any man, had seen the swift development of the affair. Silently, he blessed it, for the problem of having a stray native girl on his hands had at first given him some misgivings.

He decided that the difficulties were already in course of being solved.

But now there were other problems on his mind. After a certain amount of thought he decided that he could not turn back at this late stage. Also there was the undeniable fact that his shot at the buffalo would have been audible to the Chizman below and his gorilla guards. He motioned to N'gambi, who hurried to hi side.

"We must move from this place, N'gambi," he said. "If we do not the People of the Sun will come to find and kill us. Tell the girl and be ready to move in a minute or two."

N'gambi nodded understandingly. "It is well, *bwana,*" he answered, turning on his heel again.

Brandon reloaded his rifle magazine and thought things out. From the well he could hear the urgent notes of the silver horn. To his keen ears it was obviously coming much closer.

Then, to his horror, he heard another silver horn, this time behind him in the bush.

Whirling about, he gestured urgently to N'gambi. The headman had heard the horn and grabbed up a rifle. Now the two of them stood in front of Tsakim, their rifles at the ready. The girl cowered behind them. From the undergrowth they could hear the crashing sound of heavy bodies advancing.

Brandon realised that the sounding of the horn from below must have been a series of signals between the man below and his confederate above. The shooting would, of course, have pin-pointed the white man's position.

Brandon knew that the situation was a grave one. They could not retreat because of the edge of the well; nor could they travel far along the edge, for from the sounds they could now hear it was obvious that a long line of the gorilla guards were moving up to trap them.

When Brandon caught sight of the vanguard of the grim attackers he did not waste time, but started shooting as fast as he could lever cartridges into the breech. N'gambi, too, set about the work of slaughter with a coolness that brought a word of congratulation to Brandon's lips. He was also very surprised and gratified to see that even Tsakim had grabbed a shot-gun and was trying to load it. There was not time to show her, but he shouted instructions as he fired on the advancing gorillas. Presently

Jungle Allies

the loud explosions of the gun mingled with the sharper cracks of the rifles.

A dozen of the great gorillas fell to their guns before they saw any sign of retreat on the part of their attackers.

"We've got 'em on the run!" shouted Brandon elatedly.

"Yes, *bwana*," answered N'gambi, grinning broadly. "Now we save ourselves, yes?"

Brandon nodded, watching in silence as the gorillas vanished from sight. They were being recalled by the silver noted horn now. Perhaps it was a rallying call, thought Brandon. Whatever it was it was high time he and his two companions left the scene and found better quarters.

Hurrying as fast as the terrain would permit, he led his little party round the rim of the well in the opposite direction to that which he and Lambert had taken when they located the waterfall. The loss of Lambert weighed heavily on him now, but there was nothing he could do about it and brooding was the last thing Brandon indulged in. Besides which, his immediate difficulties were taking up all his attention.

It was clear now that they could no longer conceal their presence in the district, but by lying low they might be able to persuade the Chizmans they had gone. Accordingly, Brandon selected a well-sheltered spot and made camp for the night, which was only a few hours off by this time. Little was said, for silence was a wise quality under the circumstances.

The chosen place where they rested was very much closer to the overhanging side of the well where the dwellings were situated. Brandon hoped that he might learn something more about the place by watching on the morrow—if he could avoid detection in so doing.

It was early when he left Tsakim with N'gambi and set out to do some spying. By ten o'clock in the morning he was safely established in a concealed niche close to the edge of the well, and it was from this point that he learnt quite a lot more about the Chizmans and their culture.

The dwellings he had seen were grouped close to the sheer wall of the scrub-covered cliff. Great outcrops of rock showed through the scrub at this place, forming the over-hang.

Brandon was peering downwards at the dwellings from a distance of something like a quarter of a mile. It was from this position that he caught sight of the wicker cage for the first time. Suspended from the front wall of one of the largest of the buildings, it hung away from the wall by several feet as far as he could tell, and was at least twenty feet above the ground. Strong ropes of twisted liana strands secured it to a system of rough pulleys and counter-weights.

But the thing inside the cage was what Brandon was really interested in more than anything else.

There was definitely something alive in the cage, and it looked as if it was big enough to be a human being, but was so huddled up and crouched that it was difficult to be certain.

"Some prisoner, I suppose," mused Brandon to himself.

He looked further afield, seeing other things of interest, one of which was a stout wooden stockade in which were bunched a large number of the gorillas used as guards. They stood or sat about in apparent contentment, and once again Brandon wondered at a people who could train, tame and presumably rear the animals for their own ends. He could well see what a gold-mine of knowledge Walt C. Cochran would have found this city had he lived to find it.

Lying on his stomach in the shade of the scrub, Brandon went on watching as figures of Chizmans appeared and moved about in front of the dwellings. His interest quickened considerably when what looked like a long procession of robe-garbed men filed out through the doorway of the largest of the buildings. The procession, for that was what it obviously was, was headed by a tall, black haired giant of a man arrayed in gorgeous clothing that caught the rays of the sun as the man left the shadow of the well side and led the way into a sort of forecourt that extended for many yards along the frontage of the one-sided city.

Brandon's eyes returned to the gently swinging wicker cage then, for a shaft of sunlight that came downwards from some wedge-shaped rift in the wall of the pit was gradually throwing it into vivid relief.

A moment later the sunlight lit it squarely, revealing to the watching man's incredulous gaze the form of a white girl.

Instantly he realised that he was probably looking down at the lost Naomi Jensen. Whether the people who had captured her had been the same as the Chizmans he did not know, but the coincidence was too good to miss. It struck him, too, that he had seen among the copper-skinned Chizmans a number of blacks. Probably a subject race, he decided.

Suppose, he thought, that the Chizmans made use of some other race or tribe to do some of their dirty work outside the well? It was a feasible notion, and he now felt sure that the helpless girl in the wicker cage could be none other than the woman young Lambert had been so set on rescuing.

The fact that she was still alive was nothing to go by, for she might have been kept for some special occasion, either for sacrificial purposes or something of another nature.

The question was how could he best rescue her?

He glanced across at where the long procession of robed Chizmans were wending their way towards a circular clearing some hundred yards from the building from which hung the cage.

What he saw there brought his heart to his mouth with apprehension, for right in the centre of the little clearing a number of black skinned slaves were setting up what could only be a sacrificial altar.

Lying on the altar as they stood aside, was a long knife, its curving blade gleaming like a mirror in the sunlight. At the same time Brandon saw to his horror that the cage was being lowered to the ground by ropes.

7

LONG SHOT

WATCHING in a kind of fascinated horror, Brandon foresaw what was to happen as clearly as if he could already see the actual events.

Across at the altar the long line of Chizmans were forming up into a circle round the edge of the clearing.

From all the other buildings there appeared numbers of the copper-skinned people and their black subject race. They made their way to the clearing where the priests were waiting. Everything, it seemed, was ready for the great moment of sacrifice. All that remained was to bring along the victim for the great curved knife that was being gravely handed to the chief of the robed men around the altar.

And Brandon was watching with bated breath as the cage was lowered to the ground by three of the slaves while one of the Chizmans stood by.

It was only with a sudden physical effort that Brandon tore his gaze from these gruesome preparations and realised that unless he acted swiftly he would see the unlucky Naomi slaughtered before his gaze like a fatted calf at a feast.

"It wouldn't be possible from where I am," he muttered. "But I've got to do it somehow or other! I've just got to! She isn't going to die if I can help it."

The ghost of an idea was already forming in his mind, but whether it would work out the right way or not would depend on so many different factors that the whole thing was a long shot.

Among the articles that Brandon had been carrying on him at the time of the raft disaster was a silencer for his favourite high-velocity rifle. He had found it a useful adjunct when trying to bag more than one specimen of a herd of buck, for the fact that the killing shot was almost silent did not scare away everything within a large radius. Now he had a hunch that the silencer would prove of vital use.

Taking it from his pocket, he fitted it to his rifle with care, then began to work his way along the rim of the well till he could find a place that was ideal for covering the stone altar and the clearing that formed a gathering ground for the people of Chizma.

In the meantime he saw the white girl taken from the cage and led away towards the clearing.

The fact that she was dressed in rags and had her hands chained behind her back made him compress his mouth in a grim hard line. That these barbarous people should be able to treat a girl in such a manner was incredible. Snuggling the rifle against his shoulder and testing the line of fire, Brandon felt a faint smile of anticipation spreading across his sun-tanned features. Then it left as quickly as it had come, for the manner in which the men were driving Naomi Jensen towards the clearing raised his anger to white heat. He had great difficulty in refraining from drawing a bead on the men responsible and shooting them down, but caution forbade the action. If he succeeded in what he had in mind it would have a far greater and more lasting effect on the people against whom he had pitted himself.

Slowly and laboriously the figure of the girl was driven towards the altar. After being in the cage it was plain that she was suffering from cramp and stiffness in her legs, but no matter how she stumbled and sometimes fell on her face in the dust the men around her beat her into movement again.

At length she was close to the clearing and the circle of Chizmans who waited patiently for the moment of sacrifice. It could be nothing else for which she was being brought to the priests. Brandon recalled that these people worshipped the sun, and he knew, too, that the ancient Aztecs in their own form of sun-worship had made great play of human sacrifice. That Naomi Jensen was doomed and earmarked for such a fate was as clear as the bruises that showed up lividly on her flesh even at the distance from which he watched her progress.

Two of the priests relieved the slaves of the girl, taking charge of her themselves and leading her more gravely to the altar.

The chains were removed from her wrists. The upper parts of her ragged clothes were ripped off. Then she was lifted bodily onto the altar, to be held down with her face to the blazing sun.

The high priest, his gorgeous robes glittering in the brilliant light, picked up the sacrificial knife, holding it aloft and turning round so that everyone gathered in the clearing could see it plainly.

Then he made some mysterious signs with the long curved blade in the air.

Brandon tightened his grip on the silenced rifle in his hands. The crucial moment was coming and his tingling nerves seemed almost to cry out in an agony of suspense, so taut were they strung.

The priest stopped his movement of the knife. It was now steady, held above his head, on the point of being plunged straight into the pulsing heart of the white girl before him.

Squinting through the telescopic sight of his rifle, Brandon started squeezing the trigger. He was suddenly icy calm and absolutely collected. If he failed now the death of the girl would be on his own hands, not the priests.

The soft *plonk of* the rifle was barely audible as he fired. The range was long for the tiny target at which he aimed. But Brandon's life had hung on his own ability more than once in the past.

The priest's knife started coming down; it dropped in a slow arc at the top of the downwards drive. Then the bullet from Brandon's rifle spanked home.

The gathering of people in the clearing held their breath as the priest held his knife on high. Their eyes were riveted on the gleaming sickle blade as it began its descent.

But before it had hardly started a great gasping cry went up from the crowd.

The priest spun round, grabbing at his wrist and turning this way and that in bewildered fear.

The knife, so sacred that no one was permitted to touch it but the high priest of Chizma himself, had been snatched from his fingers in an instant.

He saw it a moment later, lying on the ground yards away, the curved blade snapped off short.

For a moment there was dead silence, then wailing cries broke out from the other priests, to be taken up by the people themselves as they saw and understood what had happened. It was a miracle; but a miracle that put more fear into the people of Chizma than anything else could have been calculated to do.

High on the edge of the wall of the great pit, Brandon lowered his rifle to the ground. The sweat was pouring down his face in streams. Every nerve and muscle in his body quivered with reaction. He dropped his head on his forearm and let his breath go with a sigh of relief that came from the deepest part of his heart.

"Done it!" he breathed in a broken whisper. "My God, I've never been so scared in my life before!"

He had literally to force himself to look again into the well, though he knew that in the face of such a miracle as the snatching of the sacrificial knife the Chizmans would not dare to carry through their present ceremony. Was it not plain enough that the gods were dissatisfied with the event? Had they not been the knife would have been allowed to finish off the life of the captured white girl.

Brandon grinned to himself as he watched the scene of dismay, bewilderment and outright fear that gripped the people in the clearing.

He was glad that his long shot had come off, for the bullet he had fired had struck the knife squarely on the blade, smashing it. The whole effect might have been ruined if his shot had wounded the priest; as it was the thing was a miracle of the finest variety.

But the girl was by no means out of trouble.

Brandon did not think they would carry through with a repeat performance immediately. It would be against their principles.

As he watched from his vantage point he saw her lifted from the altar by two of the priests. She was handled with some degree of care on this occasion. The priests led her back towards the cage. Behind them came the main crowd of Chizmans and slaves. Silence descended on the clearing. The files of people wound their way back to the buildings, gradually dispersing, though a few gathered in a group as if discussing the latest development.

Naomi Jensen was replaced in the wicker-work cage and hoisted off the ground again.

Brandon caught a glimpse of the high priest, still in his gorgeous clothing, walking slowly to and fro in front of what he took to be the temple of the cult, shaking his head very slowly and sadly from side to side. He walked with his hands clasped behind his back.

Brandon waited only for long enough to make sure that the girl was not in any immediate danger, then he hurriedly retraced his steps to the place where he had left N'gambi and the dusky Tsakim.

"N'gambi," he said quietly when the tall headman came to meet him. "N'gambi, things are moving swiftly. The white girl for whom we search is a prisoner in the well. The priests of their worship were about to make a sacrifice of her, but I managed to stop it in time. Now an attempt must be made to rescue her before they regain their courage and carry out the sacrifice tomorrow."

"When will it be, *bwana?*" N'gambi took the news calmly, as if such things as this were an everyday occurrence in his life.

Brandon thought for a moment. His glance fell on the bright eyed native girl. He guessed that a considerable amount had happened between Tsakin and N'gambi during his absence.

"They are sun worshippers, N'gambi," he murmured with a slight frown. "I do not think they would carry out their sacrifice until the sun is again in the same position as it was this morning when I watched. That is why I have returned to talk with you. It is well, for I shall be going away again and you and the girl will be alone. You must guard her with the greatest care and defend her life."

"With my own, if the *bwana* says so," answered N'gambi simply.

Brandon grinned. "Good!" he grunted. "Now let us eat a little, for I have a journey before me during which I doubt if I shall have much rest."

"What do you mean to do?"

"Enter the pit of the Chizmans as soon as possible," Brandon answered. "I shall go alone, for it is better that way. One man can move more easily than two, and there is Tsakim to think of."

"I grieve that I cannot go with you, *bwana,*" said N'gambi.

"Your turn will come later perhaps," Brandon told him.

In the meantime the native girl had busied herself with their few stores and prepared a scanty meal for the three of them. They ate in silence, listening all the time for the dreaded sound of the silver hunting horn that would call out the savage gorillas on the track of the whites.

However, nothing untoward happened to disturb Brandon's short respite from strain.

An hour after noon he was picking his way cautiously round the rim of the well, making for a place at which he could descend without being seen. It was not a simple matter, but at length he located a not-so-steep section of the scrub covered wall. By dint of slow and careful manipulation he succeeded in reaching the floor of the hundred foot deep depression.

Once down there in the dense green undergrowth he felt more at home, for there was small chance of being spotted unless he walked straight into the arms of some patrol or other. However, he did not think there were such things as patrols in this section of territory. A few gorillas perhaps, but nothing more deadly; and Brandon was in such a frame of mind at this stage that gorillas didn't worry him.

It was only the thought of Naomi Jensen that worried him. He wished more than anything that Jeff Lambert could have been spared for long enough to have taken part in her rescue. It was a pity, but he meant to do his level best to get the girl out of the tight spot in which she was. Working his way slowly through the scrub, he finally came to a place where the sound of running water was loud in his ears. Tracing it back, he saw that he was not very far from the spot at which the waterfall dropped sheer to the floor of the well. Remembering Lambert, he carried on. There was no sense in searching the dense undergrowth for the body now; not sufficient time to spare as it was, though how he was to get Naomi Jensen away from the city was something he could not work out at all as yet. Something, he told himself, would turn up. It usually did when he was faced with seemingly insurmountable obstacles.

A shallow river flowed across the well from the waterfall to some unknown exit in the opposite wall. Since Brandon could only see the immediate area around him that was all he could say.

Presently he came on another of the scattered piles of ancient masonry. The grey stone jutted up through the scrub, topping it at several points.

A sudden idea prompted Brandon to climb the weather-rotted stone and use it as a look-out point.

Raising himself up when he was level with the top of the chisel-cut stones, he discovered to his joy that he could see the buildings of the city through gaps in the foliage around him. He was considerably closer to the buildings than he had at first thought.

It was then that he realised that some intense activity was taking place in front of the buildings.

When he saw what that activity was he caught his breath in amazement, grasping his rifle more firmly and preparing himself for further action. But gradually a slow smile of comprehension spread over his face. He relaxed a little, whistling softly under his breath.

"Well I'm damned!" he muttered. "This is just about the quickest change of tactics I've ever struck in my life!"

8

GODDESS OF CHIZMA

Brandon's view of the Chizman dwellings was fairly good. He could see the hanging cage of wicker-work in which the white girl had been imprisoned.

Now the cage had been lowered to the ground again.

Naomi Jensen was no longer inside it, but was standing in the centre of a group of Chizman women, their bodies moving lithely as they tended the girl. From a distance many other people were watching, for the girl who but a short time previously had been earmarked as a human sacrifice was now being decked out in long flowing robes.

As Brandon watched one of the attendant women placed a complicated looking head-dress on Naomi's gleaming blonde hair. Her hair had been brushed so that it sparkled in the sunlight that streamed down into the deep sided well.

At first Brandon had not been able to make head or tail of what was going on, for it seemed to him completely crazy that they should be treating the unfortunate girl in this way.

But when they had finished the women of Chizma backed away from Naomi, bowing respectfully so that their heads almost touched the ground.

Naomi stood rigidly staring in front of her. Even at that distance it was obvious that she was bewildered and puzzled by this unexpected turn of events. She was also afraid, but Brandon could see that she held her head high and refused to let her captors see fear on her face.

The next development had Brandon guessing for a moment.

Followed by some of his companions, the high priest of Chizma walked slowly and proudly into the open from one of the nearby buildings. It was the building which Brandon had taken for a temple earlier on. The sound of chanting reached his ears; and in the background there was some sort of weird music being played on wind instruments.

Halting in front of the solitary white girl, the high priest bowed and touched his forehead with his hand.

To Brandon's surprise he saw Naomi Jensen incline her head in recognition of the priest's homage.

The priest gestured towards the temple building, making it plain to the girl that he wished her to enter it ahead of him. Instantly the sound of barbarous music was louder.

The girl hesitated for a moment, then began to walk very slowly towards the temple.

The priest and his acolytes followed at a respectful distance, hands folded in front of them, heads bowed.

It was not until then that Brandon fully grasped the significance of what was going on. When he did he started to grin, for it seemed a stroke of luck indeed that the people of Chizma should have put such an interpretation on his shot at the sacrificial knife. There could be no denying now that Naomi had been acclaimed a goddess.

Brandon smiled to himself when he thought about it. His smashing of the knife must have been taken as a sign by the priests that the life of the girl was sacred.

Under the circumstances this latest turn of events suited Brandon well, for he had not been able to think of any plan that was foolproof enough to ensure the rescue of the girl. Now, however, he did not think she would be in any immediate danger, and the rescue bid could safely be left until after dark, when the chances would be greatly improved.

He remained where he was for long enough to watch her lead the little procession into the temple and disappear from sight. The chanting and music gradually died away, but large crowds of Chizmans continued to stand around in front of the temple, watching and obviously hoping for another glimpse of their new white-skinned goddess.

Brandon decided the time had come to return to N'gambi and Tsakim.

Now that he knew how the land lay he might be able to make use of N'gambi for a night time attempt.

However, he was counting without the watchfulness of the Chizmans.

Hardly had he begun to climb down from his vantage point when the air was suddenly full of the warning call from the silver noted horn.

Glancing anxiously over his shoulder, he saw large numbers of the trained gorilla guards being taken from the wooden stockade and lined up in readiness to move off.

Before he was down from the pile of ruined masonry the detachment was already leaving the city, moving fast, with four of the mail-covered Chizman warriors in attendance.

"That's bad!" muttered Brandon. He knew instinctively that the guards were making for the place where N'gambi and the native girl had been left.

Turning back on his own tracks he realised with a sick sense of dismay that he must travel a much greater distance to reach his companions than the gorillas. Nor was there any means of warning them without attracting attention to himself. For the sake of the white girl he did not wish to do that, for the high priest might begin to think things out for himself.

There was nothing for it but to make what speed he could back to N'gambi.

Pressing on through the scrub and thorn that covered the bottom of the well, Rex Brandon was sweating profusely by the time he reached the place at which he had climbed down from the rim above.

The laborious clamber to the top, during which he was forced to use a certain amount of caution, seemed endless, and when he at last completed it he was close to exhaustion, for he had pushed himself remorselessly.

Lying on the rim, staring down into the jungle-choked well, he saw signs of great activity going on around the stone buildings of the Chizmans. More of the guards were being brought out from their stockades, to be lined up and moved off across the pit. There was no time to lose, he thought, and already he might be too late. N'gambi could put up a fight on his own if the need arose, but Brandon did not fancy the idea. The life of his faithful bearer was precious to him now, for their adventures had been many.

Forcing himself to carry on, he set off round the rim of the well, covering ground with surprising speed in view of the travelling conditions.

But he was still several hundred yards from the place where his two companions had been left when he heard what he dreaded most of all—the roar of gorillas, the crack of a rifle, and the notes of the horn. There was triumph in the latter sound as it reached his ears, and he knew that his effort had been insufficient.

There was just one chance, and that a slim one. N'gambi and Tsakim might not have been killed, but merely taken prisoners.

He prayed that that might be the case as he plunged on through the scrub and trees to the point where he thought he would be able to get a glimpse of the scene. Several more shots rang out before silence fell, so it was plain that N'gambi was fighting as best he could. But the odds must have been at least a hundred to one from what Brandon had seen of the strength of the gorilla cohorts.

And when at length Brandon arrived at the spot it was to find an area of flattened undergrowth, blood-stained earth and broken branches. The bodies of four gorillas lay inert on the ground. But there was no sign of N'gambi or his little companion.

"Captured!" he muttered grimly. "Well, I suppose that's better than finding them both dead!" He raised his head and peered round keenly. Then he swore to himself that nothing should be left undone if there was the slightest chance of rescuing all that remained of his safari.

Without a minute's rest, he set off once more, retracing his steps and once again entering the well where the People of the Sun held sway.

Dusk was already falling. From Brandon's point of view it might be a good thing, for it would make movement easier; but at the same time it hindered his own observation on the dwellings and houses of the distant city. Also, he did not know whether the Chizmans posted guards at night round the city. The odds were that they did, and he could not afford to take a chance on running into any of them.

In the distance he could hear the almost incessant beat of drums, the sound of chanting voices and the music he had heard during the day. At a rough guess he decided that the People of the Sun were getting ready for a feast of triumph after their recent capture.

Such a feast would bode little good for N'gambi and Tsakim, thought Brandon grimly. And he doubted if Naomi's position would be strong enough to prevent further bloodshed. Even a goddess could be ignored if it suited the priests.

Pushing his way through the tangled undergrowth on the track of the gorilla army that had taken his two companions, he foresaw a considerable amount of trouble ahead. He had his rifle, a revolver and a hunting knife for weapons, but his ammunition was limited to what he had in his belt. He would have to watch his step; there was no doubt about it.

It was when he was less than half a mile out across the floor of the well that he heard the sound of the warning call again. In the growing darkness it was eerie music, and he knew it foreshadowed another search.

They certainly had a first-class espionage system, he thought bitterly, He hadn't thought he had made all that noise coming through, but they knew he was there!

A second later, however, he was not so sure that the unwanted attention of the gorilla guards was directed at himself.

A stumbling, cracking noise in the undergrowth ahead of him made him freeze in his tracks, gripping his rifle tightly.

Than the pale-coloured bulk of a running man broke into view through the scrub not ten yards away.

Brandon raised his rifle, finger tight round the trigger.

The figure of the man halted, waving its arms and seeming on the point of turning about.

Brandon let his breath go sibilantly. He lowered his rifle and darted forward, grabbing at the man's arm and holding him firmly.

"Not so fast," he said quietly. "I didn't see you clearly at first."

The man he grasped was gagging and gasping from the wild exertion of his run. He stared up into Brandon's face with startled eyes, wide with fear and partly hidden behind the lenses of a pair of spectacles. One of the lenses was cracked right across. The nose-piece was bent.

"Who are you?" demanded Brandon. For one incredible moment he thought he had met the ghost of Jeff Lambert, but this man was short, plump and almost completely bald.

Before the man could answer something clicked in Brandon's mind;

memory stirred. His last meeting with Professor Walt C. Cochran had taken place in a luxurious New York hotel. Cochran had been smiling then, talking gaily to friends. Now he looked as if he'd been through a thorn bush backwards, and his fat round face was lined and drawn from strain.

He opened his mouth, but Brandon suddenly clapped a hand across it, listening worriedly.

Not very far away there were sounds of hasty movement in the scrub.

"Quiet!" hissed Brandon tersely. "We're getting out of this, Professor!"

Grasping the man's arm with steely fingers, he turned and headed back towards the wall of the well, half a mile distant. They made a good deal of noise in their retreat, but Brandon knew that out in the open floor of the well they would quickly be surrounded. With their backs to the wall, as it were, they would at least stand a chance of fending off attack, even if only for a time. The nearest point of the scrub-covered wall to where they were was close to the spot at which the waterfall landed.

Hurrying, the two of them forced their way through till they were brought up short by the steeply rising ground.

Brandon had been aiming at the waterfall for two reasons. Firstly, it gave him a definite direction in the darkness; and secondly, the noise of the water when they reached the vicinity of the fall would help to conceal their own movement.

But behind them they could still hear the steady advance of the Chizmans and their wild gorilla soldiers.

"We'll manage if we have any luck!" snapped Brandon. "Just you stick close to me. Professor! I'm getting to know this territory pretty well now!" He bared his teeth in a savage grin as he weighed the chances in his mind. They were better than he had at first thought, he told himself.

Cochran, who till now had not uttered a single word, gave a sigh of relief as the dark barrier of the well-side brought them to a halt.

"The waterfall," he gasped. "If we can reach it I reckon we'll be safe. I sure hope so, anyway! This place gives me the willies, and I've been dodging around, it for quite a time now."

Brandon smiled to himself at the sound of Cochran's tone. He liked the slow drawl with which the man spoke, and recalled that Walt C.

Cochran was a native of the Middle West of America.

"Plenty of time for talking presently," said Brandon. "Less noise we make the better at the moment. I'll just say I'm glad you're with me. We could have passed each other with a yard to spare and never met in this stuff."

Cochran nodded in the darkness, which was by this time complete. No glimmer of light penetrated down through the foliage of the trees above their heads.

Brandon led the way towards the waterfall, the sound of it filling his ears and giving him more confidence than ever.

He and Cochran were standing on the edge of the little torrent, peering into the darkness that surrounded them.

Brandon turned and stared back in the direction from which the gorillas might be expected to come. He did not think they were all that close, but to his horror he caught sight of a blundering shape not many yards distant.

He gripped Cochran's arm and dragged the man down behind a thicket of thorn. The bulk of the animal paused, head thrust forward searchingly. Brandon knew that even if it had not heard them it would scent them without any difficulty. Yet he did not want to shoot it, for the finding of the body when the rest arrived would give away the fact of their being close.

Cochran was tugging at his sleeve. He glanced down, to see the little fat man pointing back towards the waterfall.

They edged away, leaving the solitary gorilla still a bit baffled. Cochran knew what he was doing, and under the present circumstances Brandon was content to let him take the lead. A few minutes later he was glad he had done so, for the Professor took him right up to the stream of falling water and actually ducked down behind it.

With his lips close to Brandon's ear he said: "There's a cave in back of this trickle. We can lie up there for a while."

Brandon nodded, though his companion could not see the gesture. Then he allowed himself to be drawn into the deep black, water-splashed hole that Cochran indicated.

Together the two of them crouched just back from the cave entrance. It was a godsend that cave, for it undoubtedly saved them from detection.

Nothing could have been better as it turned out, and Brandon muttered a word of thanks as he felt Cochran close beside him in the darkness.

After what seemed a very long time he decided to take a look round outside. In spite of the darkness that had shadowed everything earlier on he knew that the moon was due to rise, had probably done so already. Even counting the thickness of the foliage some measure of light would seep down through the trees and scrub.

Leaving Cochran, he wormed his way to the entrance of the cave and peered out through the curtain of falling water, shading his eyes against the spray that jerked up at him in smooth, cool mists.

There was no sign of movement of any kind beyond the cave and he came to the conclusion that the gorillas and Chizman warriors had withdrawn disappointed, thinking that they were on the wrong track. Apparently they were not familiar with the existence of the cave or they would certainly have sent something in to investigate it. As far as Brandon was concerned it was a good thing, and the cave might yet prove a valuable hiding-place on other occasions if he was forced to remain for long in the well.

But now he was eager to make an exit and see what could be done about the problem of rescuing N'gambi, Tsakim and the unfortunate white girl who was now a goddess of the Chizman sun cult.

Returning to Cochran, he pulled him out of the cave and ducked into the cover of the scrub. When they were some distance from the waterfall and could make each other hear, he stopped again and started talking in low-pitched tones:

"I never expected to run across you alive, Professor," he said. "I came here, and was brought into the business, by young Jeff Lambert. We happened on each other on the Chuapa River, and he told me the story of your adventures."

Cochran gripped his arm. "Is that young rip alive?" he demanded urgently. "Boy, oh, boy, was he good! We were the greatest buddies ever when things began to happen!"

Brandon shook his head unhappily. "Sorry, sir," he said. "Lambert was killed when a charging buffalo took him over the edge of this pit. I couldn't save him." Cochran fell silent, head dropping forward on his chest.

"That's too bad," he said at length. "I was hoping he'd be coming around. But what brought you here? The girl? She's alive and well as far as I know, but in a pretty nasty position from what I've seen." He gave a low laugh that had little humour in it. "Me, too, for a spell, but I managed to escape."

"I thought you'd been killed by a spear," said Brandon. "That's what I understood from Lambert. He saw you go down, and then he was knocked on the head himself. When he came round you'd vanished and so had Naomi Jensen. It was just a hunch of his that the girl was still alive that drove him to try to reach civilisation. He'd have made a personal attempt to get her free but got lost in the jungle."

Cochran grunted. "Gee, that's a darned shame," he said. "I was hit by a spear; badly wounded, too, but they couldn't keep a hold on Walt C. Cochran! I was taken down to this well or whatever you call it and caged up like the girl. They tended my wound for some reason of their own and then I managed to escape. I've been roaming about down here ever since. They nearly had me more than once, and if I'd been armed with anything I'd have tried to get the girl loose. As it was…"

Brandon nodded. "I am armed," he pointed out, "and I mean to rescue Naomi if it's humanly possible. Lambert was dead set on the idea, but he didn't live long enough to take a hand. Now it's you and I, Professor!"

Cochran gave a sigh that was partly relief and partly worry. "We've sure got a job on our hands!" he observed.

Brandon nodded in the gloom. He stood up and began to move on towards the town of the Chizmans. It was then that the monstrous shapes of gorillas rose up in front of them, on both sides and in their rear. They were surrounded.

9

CONDEMNED!

THE fight in the darkness was short. Though Brandon and his companion put up what effort they could the result was a foregone conclusion. With only a rifle and one revolver between them—which Brandon thrust into Cochran's hand—they were no match against the hordes that pressed in on them from all sides in the thick undergrowth.

Brandon saw several of the animals and their human attendants go down before his bullets. Cochran, too, accounted for more than one with the revolver. But soon the magazines of both their weapons were empty and they were given no respite in which to reload.

As Brandon fired his last shot and clubbed the rifle a brawny Chizman whirled in to the attack, bearing him backwards with a vicious blow from the flat of a broad-bladed sword.

From the corner of his eye he caught a glimpse of Cochran locked in the hairy embrace of one of the gorillas. Then deepest blackness enveloped his brain as someone struck him down from behind in a numbing concussion that collapsed him like a pricked balloon. The only thought in his mind at the moment was why they had not both been killed outright as he had fully expected.

When he next opened his eyes he was no longer fighting in the darkness of the jungle, but realised he was cramped up on the ground with his arms and legs securely tied. The sky above him was dark, but all round was the flickering light of hundreds of flaring torches. The flames were reflected on the grey stone walls of buildings, so that he guessed he had been carried to the city. The notion gave him much food for thought. Craning his neck around painfully, he discovered that the pot-bellied figure of Walt C. Cochran was lying on the ground within a couple of feet of his own position. From the look of the professor Cochran was still out for the count.

Brandon shifted slightly so that his view of his surroundings was widened a little.

It was then that he caught sight of N'gambi and Tsakim. The very sight of them warmed his heart, for he had feared that they might already be dead after being captured. However, it seemed that they were being saved up for some ceremonial sacrifice, for, like Naomi Jensen when Brandon had first seen her, N'gambi and Tsakim were installed in wicker-work cages that hung about twenty feet above the ground in front of one of the buildings. They were some thirty yards from where he himself and Professor Cochran were lying.

Standing guard over the two prisoners were a dozen of the stalwart Chizman warriors.

Brandon decided to feign unconsciousness for a time until he saw what was happening. It was obvious that a feast was in progress, for the sound of wind instrument music and sullen-sounding drums was loud in the air. Turning his head to the right he was able to keep an eye on the entrance to the temple. Naomi Jensen had disappeared inside it when he last saw her. He wondered if she was still inside.

There was no way of telling, however, but before long he had plenty of interest to occupy his attention.

From the temple door there appeared a long procession of priests and their attendants, followed by scantily-clad, women who moved as if their feet were on air, gliding along with all the natural grace of the East. They were suddenly out of place in this barbarous country, so that Brandon wondered what manner of people the Chizmans were, and what stock they came from in the past. It was a puzzle which probably Cochran could have solved, but Brandon could only make guesses—and guesses were of little use in his present predicament.

Following the women, came an ornate litter borne by four of the tall Chizman warriors. They were arrayed in chain mail, with broad-bladed swords at their waists and long spears in their free hands. Moving with an easy stride, they carried the litter out through the entrance of the temple.

Seated on the litter was an old Chizman nobleman. At first glance it was difficult to tell his age, but he was considerably older than those around him, and his hair was almost white, whereas the prevailing colour of his fellow people was black. But the keen, cruel features were typically Chizman in cut and look.

As he appeared on his litter the gathering of guards and citizens bowed low to the ground, touching their foreheads in a sort of mute homage.

The old man on the litter made no sign that he was even aware of their existence. The music of the wind instruments took on a different, subtly flattering note to their cadence.

Brandon, watching intently, realised that this old man could be none other than the ruler of the city. There was about him a regal air that nothing could conceal. The music, the drums, the flaring light of the torches seemed to intensify the illusion. Brandon could feel it as if it was a solid thing, a rather frightening thing.

And he saw, too, that the procession and the litter was making towards them, winding from the temple entrance with slow, grave steps.

It was at that moment that a voice reached Brandon's ears and made him look sharply across at Professor Cochran.

The American anthropologist had recovered and was staring in the direction of the procession, just as Brandon was. The guards around them made no move to prevent them watching, so that Brandon did not think it worthwhile pretending insensibility any longer.

"That's the king of this outfit," muttered Cochran in a quiet aside.

"So I gathered," Brandon answered. "He's rather a grand looking old boy, isn't he?"

Cochran grunted quietly. "You'll think so when we're hauled in front of him," he said. "They're as cruel as any living race I've ever come across in all my natural!"

Brandon nodded uncomfortably. He had already reached that conclusion from what he had seen of the city of Chizma and its methods of treating prisoners.

"Where do these queer people spring from?" he inquired.

Cochran was silent for a moment or two. The procession was close to them by this time; in a minute or two the litter would be lowered to the ground and the guards would bring the prisoners before their ruler. Brandon guessed all this; Professor Cochran already knew it for fact. He had been a captive of the Chizmans before, and the routine was not new.

"As far as I've been able to decide the Chizmans are an off-shoot of the ancient group of races from which the Aztecs originally came," said Cochran slowly. "The whole thing is something of a mystery of course, and requires intensive study before we can be sure of our facts, but that is my own opinion after this enforced stay with them."

"Very interesting," commented Brandon dryly.

The procession had by this time halted some twenty yards from where they were lying on the ground. As it did so the guards around them closed in and dragged them roughly to their feet, hustling them forward towards the litter where it rested in the midst of the four bearers.

Held firmly upright on their tied feet, Brandon and the professor were brought to a stop close to the litter.

The old man on it peered at them narrowly in the uncertain light of the torches. His eyes, though old, were keen and bright with some inner light that was mostly cruel.

Then he said something in a high-pitched, cracked voice. Who it was addressed to Brandon could not guess, nor did he understand the language.

Glancing at Cochran, he raised his eyebrows wonderingly.

"He's condemning us to death," said Cochran. "I've managed to pick up a little of their lingo since I was held prisoner."

The old man said something more, the hard, finely-chiselled lines of his face revealing a cruelty in his nature that was almost ghoulish. Brandon could not help shuddering, though the actual meaning of what he said was lost on him.

Looking at Cochran again, he saw that the fat professor was visibly paler and more drawn looking than he had been a moment before.

"What is it now?" demanded Brandon tersely. "You look worried."

Cochran gave a start as if brought back to earth with a jolt. "So would you be if you could understand!" he said. "We're to be killed. He's condemned us to death without any appeal, but it's not that so much that worries me as the way they mean to do it."

"How's that?" Brandon's voice was hard-edged and ragged with strain.

"Take it easy, son," advised the professor gently. "We shall need all our guts before we're through. The old man says we're to meet our death in the Pit of Lions."

"Oh..." Brandon shuddered at the words, but he held himself stiffly in the grip of the guards. The People of the Sun would never be able to say that a white man had shown himself afraid in their midst.

"We'll make out all right, you'll see," he grated to the professor. "Not dead yet by a very long way!"

"That's the stuff!" answered Cochran. He looked at the ruler squarely, meeting the stare of the cold eyes with defiance.

"What's he saying?" asked Brandon, for the regal old man was chattering away once more, laying the law down in no uncertain manner.

Cochran blinked in the dim light. "Only that until the time comes for our decease we shall be kept in cages like the others." He gave a brief laugh. "They take their time about things here, Brandon! You'll learn that if we live long enough!"

Brandon grunted. Before he could say anything more the guards who held them jerked them around arid started to drag them off. Meanwhile the litter was raised from the ground and the procession moved on, bearing the ruler of Chizma out of sight in the torch-lit gloom of night.

Hustled away towards the wicker-work cages, Brandon and Professor Cochran fell silent, for they had all their work cut out to avoid falling as they stumbled along between their guards. With their feet tied it was more a matter of moving in a series of hops than walking, of course, which was not the easiest method of progress to use.

"I'll be darned glad when this is over," grunted Cochran presently. "These devils can make a man's life hell if they get a chance."

"You worry too much!" said Brandon with a grin. "Look at poor old Lambert. He isn't even alive; whereas we at least have the pleasure of breathing air. It's the girl I'm worried about. They made her a goddess, you know."

"Good Lord, did they really?" exclaimed Cochran. "Then I suppose she's lucky in a way. They hold their priests and suchlike in very high esteem here." He broke off. "But I thought they intended to use her as a special sacrifice?"

Brandon grunted agreement. "So they did!" he said. "I watched as they were about to kill her. Lucky shot of mine tore the sacred knife out of the high priest's hand and saved her. They must have accepted it as an omen or something; anyhow, the next time I spotted her she was being done up in robes and dressed as a goddess."

"I thought something of the kind was going on," said Cochran.

They might have said other things between them but by that time they were being squeezed into the none-too-large wicker cages. Next minute they were hoisted from the ground to hang suspended above the crowded scene below. There were four of the cages all told. Brandon and Cochran were three or four yards apart. Then N'gambi and Tsakim were a little further along, within speaking distance. Brandon made haste to let his headman know that he was unharmed, but that that was all they could expect for the moment.

"We, too, are well, *bwana,*" replied N'gambi. "It was a good fight while it lasted, and my Tsakim killed one of the gorillas herself. But we were outnumbered and had to give in or lose our lives."

"I'm glad you didn't fight to the death," said Brandon. "The future isn't too rosy, of course, but it might be a lot worse than it is. Tell Tsakim how sorry I am to have let her in for this."

"*Bwana,*" replied N'gambi quietly, "you need not fear that she blames you for our danger. She admires you and would follow you anywhere, for you saved her life."

Brandon said nothing. He wondered what was going to turn up to save the lives of all of them this time. They certainly needed a miracle pretty badly from the look of things.

"If you take my advice for what it's worth, Brandon," put in the professor calmly, "you'll get some rest if you can. I don't know when the show is due to begin, but *we* shall be the main attraction." He laughed. "I wouldn't want to be a disappointment to our friends the

Chizmans!"

"You have a hell of a nerve for an anthropologist!" retorted Brandon, grinning in the semi-darkness.

Cochran could not see the expression, but the tone of Brandon's voice brought a grim smile to his podgy face. He stretched as much as he could in his cramped cage and tried to find some rest for his weary, bruised body.

Brandon, too, an old campaigner, realised that if he was to acquit himself well in the coming hours of trouble he would be wise to gain all the strength he could. There was one small but important fact always before him. He did not mention it to his companions, and its usefulness when the time came for him to face the lions in the pit would depend on any number of circumstances. However, it was something to have even one trick up his sleeve.

The night wore on uncomfortably for the captives. It was not until almost dawn when the long, torch-bearing line of priests and acolytes returned from beyond the city. The old ruler was still seated on his litter, as straight and un-weary looking as when he had condemned them to death.

Brandon, who found it almost impossible to sleep, was awake at once when the first sounds of the return reached his ears. Watching closely, he could tell nothing from the procession beyond the fact that they had been beyond the city limits. What their purpose had been he could not even guess.

When the procession and the crowds had dispersed the prisoners relaxed again into fitful rest. The wicker-work of the cages into which they were crammed destroyed the idea of comfort completely. Brandon felt as if every bone in his body was sticking out through his flesh by the time the sky was above the well gradually flushed with the coming dawn.

"Mornin', Professor!" he called across to Cochran's cage. "Had your breakfast yet? What's the service like in this place?"

"Lousy!" answered Cochran in an irritable tone. "I haven't eaten; I shan't eat; and the service, as you call it, is terrible! You'd better put in a complaint to the Belgian Government when we're through!"

Brandon laughed loudly, causing several early Chizmans to glance up at the wicker-work cages in amazement.

"Do your own dirty work!" he retorted good-naturedly to Cochran. "But seriously, do they feed us at all?"

"I wouldn't be alive now if they didn't," answered the professor tersely. "Still, the fare isn't all that hot—when you get it, which isn't very often. Look how thin I've gone!"

Brandon laughed. "Don't kid yourself, Professor!" he said.

Brandon talked for a short while with N'gambi after that, then silence fell between them, for the city was waking and their natural curiosity got the better of them. Also, they were none of them in as high spirits as they pretended to make out.

Presently, two of the Chizman guards appeared with large bowls of sloppy looking stew. The cages were lowered to the ground one after the other and the stew was ladled out into gourds, one each for the prisoners.

When Brandon first tasted his portion he thought he would be sick, but the others seemed to relish the unsavoury stuff.

Cochran shouted down to one of the guards when the cages were raised again.

Though Brandon could not understand a word of what was said he guessed that Cochran was questioning the man.

At the end of the brief conversation the professor gave a shrug and turned to Brandon.

"What did you learn?" inquired Brandon curiously. "I wish I could make out their language. I thought I had a smattering of most of the African dialects, but this one has me beaten."

"It would," replied Cochran. "It isn't African in any event; but that wasn't what I had to say. The big show these boys are putting on is due to take place tonight when the moon comes up. I gather that it should have been staged at full moon a few nights ago, but the white girl was not quite ready for sacrifice then, so they put it off. Then they discovered she wasn't intended to die in any case, so they made her a goddess and the show tonight is to be in her honour." He grinned crookedly. "Pretty little scheme, isn't it?"

"Very!" grunted Brandon. "So now we know, eh? All day to wait, and part of the night as well."

Cochran nodded somewhat gloomily.

But N'gambi called across to Brandon: "*Bwana,*" he said, "it may be that we shall escape before we die, in which good event, the night is of much assistance to a running man."

Brandon nodded thoughtfully. He was glad that the tall, broad-shouldered headman was not giving up hope. Nor was Tsakim, for she and N'gambi chattered together a great deal during the course of the morning. On more than one occasion Brandon caught the sound of her laugh, soft and musical as she listened to something N'gambi said. He was thankful that the two had found each other, even if their pleasure was to last for only a short time. With the growing day the heat increased till the captives fell silent. Their present position was fully exposed to the burning rays of the sun, and none of them had a scrap of shade. For the blacks it was not as bad as it might have been, but Brandon and the professor found it distinctly uncomfortable. In fact, they were glad enough when the sun went down below the rim of the well and brought a measure of coolness to their sweating bodies.

"Thank the Lord for that!" muttered Brandon. "Now at least we shan't be fried any longer!"

He looked around him, his eyes screwed up against the bright light, though now it had lost its fierceness.

During the entire day he had not seen or heard anything of the white girl who was somewhere inside the temple building. From Cochran's further questioning of one of the guards who brought them food in the late afternoon he learnt that Naomi was in the temple, but was being kept strictly alone as a sort of preparation for her reign as goddess of Chizma.

And then came the darkness of night, bringing with it the gathering groups of people, the herding of the gorillas into their stockades, the chanting of unseen singers and the beat of muffled drums. Torches were lighted below in the open. It was plain that the People of the Sun were fully expecting a great occasion that night. They came out from houses, halls, every building in the place except the temple. The distant music of wind instruments and horns rose in the air.

Once, though he could not be certain against the background of general noise, Brandon thought he heard the far off roar of a lion.

He remembered the Pit of Lions to which they would presently be taken. His heart sank within him, but he drew a deep breath and determined to sell his life dearly when the time at last came. It might not be tonight, he thought.

Just as the moon was creeping up over the rim of the well a long procession appeared from the entrance of the temple building. It was a similar one to that which the prisoners had seen previously, but on this occasion the seat of honour was shared. The cruel-faced ruler of Chizma sat side by side with a pale and defiant-looking white girl.

Naomi Jensen, Goddess of Chizma, would watch the captives die in the Pit of Lions.

10

The Lion Pit

BRANDON watched the procession moving away from the city with a sense of dismay. He wished he could get some message of reassurance to the girl, but there was nothing he could do; and anyway, how could he reassure her when his own plight was so parlous? It was a grim prospect whichever way he looked at it.

But worse was to come.

Hardly had Brandon seen the litter with Naomi disappear through the undergrowth at the fringe of the city clearing before guards lowered the wicker-work cages to the ground.

"This looks like it, Brandon, my boy!" said Professor Cochran simply. "Don't take it too hard. We've all had a pretty full life I should say."

"We haven't finished yet!" snapped Brandon dryly as his guards dragged his cramped, stiff form from the cage and tied his hands behind his back. All the prisoners had been free to go without bonds while they were in the cages. Had they not been able to move hand or foot they would all have been dead from stiffness long before now.

"No, perhaps you're right," said Cochran. "I'm letting this thing get me down more than somewhat I'd say! You're the doctor, Rex! Just what the forces of despair need to rout 'em, eh?"

Brandon managed a grin, but he was far from feeling in the mood for humour. In fact it seemed to him that making a joke of danger under these circumstances was something of a crime. Had it not been for the position of the white girl it would not have mattered; but the plight of Naomi made him sweat even to think about.

The prisoners found themselves close together for the first time. Tsakim and N'gambi were standing side by side, their faces grave but their eyes bright with determination.

"N'gambi," said Brandon quietly as the four of them were herded away from the base of the building in more or less the same direction as that taken by the procession a few minutes before. "N'gambi, if we do not die fighting these people will laugh at the bravery of white men and their friends, the black. You and your brave woman, Tsakim, have been very dear friends to me. I should grieve deeply to lose you."

"*Bwana*," answered N'gambi soberly, "if it is the wish of the gods we shall die; but if they decide to spare our lives we shall live. I am afraid; and so is Tsakim, but you need not fear that we shall let these people see our fear. We are proud to die with you, *bwana*, but it is a pity that we cannot hunt together much longer, for we have always been happy."

Brandon swallowed hard. He shot a glance at the small black-skinned naked girl at N'gambi's side. Her woolly head was held as stiffly as if she was carved from stone.

"Tsakim," he murmured, as they were hurried along a path through the scrub, "I am sorry for this."

"It is no time for sorrow," she replied in a soft voice. "There are times when a woman would gladly die with a man."

Brandon saw her look swiftly at N'gambi. He clenched his teeth and fell silent.

Their way lay through moon-lit glades of thorn and baobab trees. When at length they reached an area lighted by the gleam of torches, Brandon saw literally hundreds of the Chizmans gathered in what appeared to be a large circular clearing.

Then the deep-throated roar of a lion came to them from the darkness beyond the ring of flaring lights.

"Sounds a healthy young creature," commented Cochran.

Brandon did not have the heart to reply. A lane was opened up in the ring of people. The prisoners and their escorting Chizman warriors passed between ranks of cruel-faced men and women. Some of the women jeered at them, but the whites took little notice. As for N'gambi and the native girl, Brandon was astounded to see them both spit in a contemptuous fashion as they were hustled on their way. It was a gesture of defiance that did him good to witness.

Then the dreaded Pit of Lions was before them. The guards came to an abrupt halt, standing as if waiting further orders from their ruler, who was seated a few yards distant.

Beside him, the two of them on a raised dais, was Naomi Jensen, drawn looking and plainly miserable in all her finery.

Brandon's heart went out to the solitary white girl as he stared at her with unashamed admiration. He could well understand Jeff Lambert's feelings for her now that he was seeing her closely for the first time. She was a beautiful woman. No more could be said.

The ruler gestured to one of his personal attendants who stood close behind him. The man in turn issued orders to the guards.

Brandon did not understand what was said, but Cochran muttered that they were not all to enter the pit at the same time. He had gathered from what was said that the ruler had decreed that the two black servants should be kept back as sport for a later session—when the white strangers had provided the people with entertainment.

"So they're splitting us up, are they?" grunted Brandon. He did not know whether to be glad or sorry. There was not a lot he could do personally to save the situation in any case, so he might as well make the best of it.

"Yes, that's the way of it, son," commented Cochran in a sober tone of voice. "Frankly, I'm scared, but I can't help it!"

"We're all scared, Professor! Who wouldn't be?"

"Maybe the devil himself," came the quick answer.

Brandon watched as N'gambi and Tsakim were taken off into the darkness out of sight beyond the clearing. He managed to say a word of farewell to his two faithful friends, but their going left him with a strangely empty feeling inside him. It was rather like waving goodbye to some important part of himself.

Then he and Cochran were thrust forward roughly till they stood on the very edge of a circular pit.

For the first time Brandon saw what they were up against.

The Pit of Lions was roughly fifteen yards in diameter. A crude wooden ladder gave access to the floor of it, which was dark with what Brandon took to be the blood of earlier victims. On the far side was a gated tunnel entrance. He guessed that the lions themselves were imprisoned behind the wooden bars, for there was a rope by which the gate could be raised to let them out into the pit.

"Surely they aren't going to toss us down there without untying us?" gasped Cochran blankly. "There wouldn't be much sport in watching that sort of thing!"

"They'll have their sport all right, don't you worry!" retorted Brandon grimly. The guard at his back was already cutting his hands free; then his legs were untied and he was free to stand and move without hindrance.

The pit, as they stood on the rim, was about ten feet deep. An agile man could have leapt up and grasped the edge of the rim to haul himself up out of reach of the lions. But the Chizmans took care of everything. That was part of the sport, obviously, for a complete circle of Chizman warriors stood at positions all around the pit, their spears pointing downwards. If a man forced himself through fear to jump for his life he would only run against the keen points of the blades.

"A barbarous race," murmured Cochran grimly.

"They've got to have their fun!" said Brandon.

Next moment he and the portly professor were being prodded to the top of the short ladder leading down to the floor of the pit. Brandon went first; then came Cochran. He was puffing and blowing from the exertion when he at last reached the ground and stood beside Brandon.

Brandon glanced round, saw that no lion had as yet been released to devour them, and then turned to face the raised dais on which the ruler of Chizma and Naomi Jensen were seated.

The girl's face showed nothing but utter misery and fear. Then a kind of sick horror spread over her features as Brandon watched them, fascinated, in the flickering light of the torches. He would have liked to have said something to her; given her some encouragement to lift her spirits, but there seemed so little he could say that he did not speak.

Cochran's face hardened as he followed Brandon's gaze. Uninhibited by any such considerations as his companion's, he inclined his head gravely in the direction of the girl. Then his drawling voice echoed across the Pit of Lions:

"See they got me again, kid," he said. "It was too bad I couldn't get you out of this jam, but I guess I'm not the strong man type."

The girl half rose to her feet, her hands clenched tightly in an agony of misery as she realised that soon she must sit and watch her old friend, the professor, torn to bits by savage wild animals.

One of the ruler's acolytes placed a firm hand on her shoulder and pressed her down into her seat again.

The hard-faced ruler at her side turned his head and shot her a glance that seemed to still any spirit she might have had to fight back.

"It's no good," grunted Brandon. "They've got the girl cold. We can only—" He broke off abruptly as a rattling sound reached his ears.

Whirling round, the two men watched in a kind of bleak fascination as the wooden bars of the gateway on the far side of the pit were drawn upwards, to reveal a black hole through which gleamed a pair of yellow eyes.

"This is it!" muttered Walt C. Cochran. "Goodbye, Rex, if I don't get another chance. It's sure been nice knowing you, son!"

He stood his ground as the big-maned lion bounded from the gaping hole that housed it. With bared fangs and roars echoing eerily and terrifyingly through the night, the animal hurled itself forward at the two men.

"Don't move!" snapped Brandon to Cochran. "I've been keeping something up my sleeve!"

As he spoke he whipped out a hunting-knife that had been inside his shirt at the time of his capture. It had been a pure stroke of luck that their captors had not discovered it, but as soon as he found out that he still had it his spirits had risen considerably. Now it might well prove the difference between life and death.

Cochran hesitated, half turned away as if to throw himself aside out of the path of the charging lion.

Drums beat furiously above on the rim of the pit. The people gathered round the arena were yelling encouragement to the animal.

The lion, a young, healthy, hungry specimen of forest breed, made straight for Cochran.

Brandon dropped to one knee, keeping his knife out of sight until the last possible moment. Then he shouted to Cochran to jump for it and hurled himself into the path of the lion in the same breath. His hand and arm shot out straight, the keen tip of the blade aimed directly at the animal's throat as it leapt for Cochran.

Cochran gasped, threw himself sideways at the last moment. Brandon felt his arm jarred from wrist to elbow as he met the onslaught of the lion. The blade of the hunting-knife entered the animal's neck, buried to the hilt. Then the lion was screaming in fury and pain, lashing out with its claws and teeth, seeking to bite his arm through in a single blow.

Somehow or other Brandon managed to avoid the terrible fangs, dragging out the knife and stepping backwards in the nick of time as the savage creature roared defiance and sprang once again.

He met the attack with a calmness that amazed even himself. Cochran yelled at him to be careful. The lion heard the shout, turned its head for an instant and shot a venomous roar at the professor.

"Get him while I attract his attention!" shouted the professor. "That's your only chance, son!"

Brandon gritted his teeth. He knew that he was now engaged in a life-and-death struggle with the creature. If he slipped or missed a blow with the knife it would be all up with both himself and his companion in trouble.

"Turn your back and run like hell!" he said between his teeth. "Do as I say! If I fail it'll be too bad!" Cochran turned on his heel without hesitation, putting his undefended back towards the lion.

The lion forgot Brandon for a few seconds. He only saw the exposed back of the professor.

Whirling round in its own length, the creature launched itself in pursuit of what it took to be an easier victim than the man with the knife.

It was Brandon's chance and he knew that he must on no account miss it.

Leaping after the lion, he took a flying jump and landed astride the animal's back.

The lion roared and tried to turn, but Brandon twisted his fingers in the tangled mane that grew thickly at its throat and shoulders. With his other hand he plunged the knife deep in the lion's throat.

It might have been all over in that moment of triumph had not the lion pulled a trick of its own.

Instead of rearing up backwards as Brandon had half expected it to, it rolled over sideways, pinning Brandon down with the full weight of its sinewy body.

"Kill it! Kill it quickly!" shouted Cochran in an agony of suspense as he saw his companion going down and being rolled over with the lion. The animal's mane was red with its own blood now where it streamed from wounds in its neck and throat. But none of them were fatal. There was still plenty of strength in the massive shoulders, and that strength and power would be used to tear Brandon limb from limb in a few short moments.

Cochran rushed in, meaning to fight with his bare hands if he had nothing else. Brandon had lost his knife in his roll with the lion. Cochran tried to snatch it up from where it had fallen from the creature's throat, but a sudden vicious slashing motion of its forelegs kicked the knife out of reach. The professor stumbled and almost fell on top of the lion. Brandon was fighting for his life, his steel-hard fingers buried in the hairy mane of the lion. But he could not possibly hope to hold the animal off for long.

With a sinking heart he felt the beast's fetid breath fanning his cheeks as the lion wormed around and got on top of him, its claws raking the flesh from his thighs in the effort. He hung on as if his very life depended on it, but the animal's strength was enormous. Its blood was dripping down on to him, soaking his bush shirt and chest in warm gushes. He brought up his knees and kicked out as hard as he could against the lion's belly, but that only seemed to make it even more savage.

An instant later he knew he was done. All the power seemed to be sapped from his arms. His muscles burned with the strain. The lion's great head was coming down towards him, dimly seen now in the torch light and the swimming senses within his own aching head.

He bit his lip till the blood flowed down his chin, then the lion's jaws were gaping only inches from his throat.

11

Flash Magic!

The blood was pounding in Brandon's ears; his teeth were clenched as he closed his eyes, knowing that his strength was gone and the lion now had him at its mercy. Professor Cochran sprang towards the animal, beating at it and kicking it to turn its attention from Brandon. But the creature only snarled at his puny efforts. Nothing but a miracle could save Brandon's life. Neither of them thought there was much chance of that.

Already torn and bleeding, Brandon lay almost inert beneath the snarling animal as it crouched over his body, roaring defiantly as if challenging anyone who dared to take his victim from him.

Brandon saw dimly that the people round the edge of the pit were in a fury of delight.

He saw Naomi cover her face with her hands, dropping her head forward to shut out the dreadful sight. The breath of the lion was hot on his face. With a short, tortured prayer on his lips Brandon gave up the last remaining shreds of hope. This was not an age of miracles, and the man knew it well enough—or thought he did. The lion's head came down, jaws gaping open, slavering and savage. He closed his eyes again, finished.

But just as he thought the great fangs must tear at his throat the body of the lion went stiff for an instant.

At the same time Brandon felt, rather than heard, a dull thud. It seemed to run through the body of the animal, communicating itself to the man beneath it. Then the lion gave a choking bellow of pain, lashed out viciously with all its broad pads and rolled over on its side.

"Get up!" shouted Cochran urgently. "Get up, man! Someone killed it!"

Brandon opened his eyes, staring round blankly. The first thing he saw was the great yellow body of the lion not a yard from where he lay. There was a long, feather-tipped arrow sticking straight up from behind the animal's shoulder.

Brandon staggered to his feet, weak and bleeding. He realised in a kind of daze that an expert marksman had killed the lion. Its death had been none too soon.

"My God!" he breathed in a broken whisper.

"Sure was a close thing, Rex!" grunted Cochran. He was grasping Brandon's arm, holding him steady.

All round the rim of the pit faces were staring down at them. Fists were being waved angrily. The voices of the Chizmans rose in fury at being cheated of their sport.

"Let's get out of here!" urged Cochran. Brandon gave a thin smile. "Easier said than done!" he muttered. "Still, we can try."

Together, he and Cochran sprinted for the side of the pit. Brandon leapt upwards, calling on all his reserves of strength to do it. The mystery of the unknown killer of the lion had him guessing, but that could be sorted out later on. It didn't matter now. The main thing was to escape if they possibly could.

But the Chizmans had no intention of letting their prey slip through their fingers.

At the rim of the pit Brandon and the professor were met by the viciously-wielded butt ends of spears. The entire place was ringed about with warriors. There was no escape!

Brandon dropped back, his face and shoulders bruised by the stabbing blows of the spear butts.

"No good!" he rasped to Cochran.

The professor nodded grimly. Staring upwards in the torch-lit gloom, he saw no trace of mercy on any of the faces that peered back at him. Listening to the babble of voices he translated for Brandon's benefit.

"They say there are plenty more lions!" he jerked. "It seems a pity, son, but it looks as if we're in for the high jump in spite of our unknown friend with the bow and arrow!"

Brandon said nothing. He felt exhausted, and his legs seemed to be made of water. Only with the greatest difficulty did he manage to stand upright and glare back at the hard-faced ruler and his barbarous people. The ruler made a brief gesture with his right hand. Instantly there was a rattle from the far side of the pit. Brandon and Cochran whirled about, to see a second lion loping towards them at a run. They separated, so that for a moment the animal could not make up its mind which man to attack. Brandon caught sight of his hunting-knife on the ground a few feet away. As the lion hurled itself at Cochran he dived for the knife, scooping it up and carrying through in a wild and desperate run for the creature.

The lion hit Cochran full in the chest, bowling him over and over on the ground.

Brandon staggered blindly on, determined to do what he could to get the animal before it killed Cochran.

But the lion sensed the danger that was coming up behind.

It pivoted round, reared up on its hind legs and struck out at Brandon, knocking the knife from his grasp before he could use it.

Brandon himself just escaped the vicious blow of the lion's forepaws. The animal thumped to the ground again and crouched on its haunches. Meanwhile the din from the watching people rose louder and louder as they yelled their approval of the show.

Brandon dropped to one knee, ready to throw himself to one side or the other as the creature dictated. Although he could barely make his muscles do as he wanted the instinct for self-preservation was so strong that not until he collapsed would he give up fighting.

Cochran failed to rise. Brandon saw him from the corner of his eye and swore softly beneath his breath. The plump professor had been winded by his fall. Brandon could not expect any assistance from that direction. If he was to save his life and that of his friend he must do it by his own unaided efforts.

But the chances of success were remarkably slim.

The savage lion, an older, tougher specimen than its predecessor, turned and launched its powerfully-muscled body at Brandon.

Brandon side-stepped clumsily. The lion struck him on his right hip and hurled him to the ground, where he lay dazed and weak, unable to rise.

The lion had him at its mercy now. It sprang round and approached him more slowly.

Brandon was again staring death in the face.

He averted his eyes, peering upwards to the star-dotted sky, knowing fear for one of the few times in his life.

The moon, a monstrous globe of yellow-white, looked down on the grim scene.

Then Brandon saw a peculiar thing.

Arcing through the sky above, dropping swiftly downwards, was a shining ball of bright red light. It was followed a moment later by another ball of fire, this time green.

With a hissing sound the first glowing ball dropped to the ground just behind the first ranks of the watching people round the rim of the pit.

Screams of dismay and fear rose in the air.

The lion, on the point of springing on Brandon for the kill, paused. It was during that pause that the second flaming light fell right into the lion pit.

The lion gave a growling snarl and backed away from the man on the ground. It ran round the pit, terror of the unknown raising the mane on its neck and shoulders.

Brandon crawled painfully to his feet.

Peering upwards, he was astonished to see that the people of Chizma were turning and fleeing from the edge of the rim. Yet another of the glowing balls of fire was arcing towards them.

Cries of terror rang loud in his ears. He glanced swiftly at Professor Cochran, to see the man struggling to his feet.

"Come on!" he yelled impatiently. "Now's our chance!"

Suiting his action to his words, he darted forward, grasped the professor by the arm and dragged him to the edge of the lion pit. The lion gave a savage roar, backing away even further. Then it spotted the entrance through which it had entered the pit. With a snarl of fear it leapt for the gated opening, disappearing through it in a flurry of dust. Its snarls echoed hollowly in the darkness beyond the entrance.

Jungle Allies

Brandon and Cochran reached the side of the pit.

Brandon made a step for Cochran with his hands and heaved the man upwards. This time there was no one to prevent them leaving the pit. Panic had broken loose above.

With Cochran up, Brandon called on the last of his strength and heaved himself up, falling forward on his face as Cochran knelt beside him.

They had left the pit on the opposite side to where the ruler and Naomi Jensen were sitting.

Twenty yards away, they could see the broken ranks of the Chizmans, running away in fright.

As if to complete the rout, there were suddenly a number of vivid flashes among the trees at the edge of the clearing. These brought forth renewed screams of fear from the people.

"The girl!" gasped Brandon. "We've got to get her away now. It's our only chance!"

He and Cochran staggered round the rim of the pit. The ruler had disappeared, fleeing with the remainder of his people, they supposed. There was now only Naomi Jensen and the high priest at the litter that had rested on the raised dais of the grandstand. Brandon shouted encouragement as he saw that the white girl was struggling bravely in an effort to escape from the grasp of the high priest. The man was powerful, but the girl fought with a desperation that stopped him from succeeding at once.

The two of them were swaying on the dais, locked in each other's arms. Naomi was kicking and scratching, her robes ripped half off her body as the priest bared his teeth and sought to keep a grip on her.

Brandon reached them a yard or two ahead of Cochran. He was gasping for breath, but knew that before long the priest would overcome the struggling girl and carry her off. There was no time to be lost. Soon, too, the remainder of the Chizmans would regain their courage and return. When that happened all chance of escape would be gone for good.

Brandon seized the high priest by the shoulders and jerked him round, smashing a blow into his evil face with all the power in his shoulders.

Naomi, breaking free of the man's grip, threw herself sideways, collapsing on the ground with a sobbing cry as she realised who her rescuers were.

Then Cochran was kneeling beside her, urging her to rise and escape.

Meanwhile. Brandon and the high priest were fighting for mastery. The Chizman was fresh and untiring, but Brandon, though close to exhaustion, was a more powerful man. In the end he got the priest down, leapt on to his chest and grabbed his long, black hair, beating his head on the earth till the priest went limp.

Rolling clear, Brandon glanced round, to see that Cochran and the girl were already running side-by-side for the cover of the nearby trees and scrub.

From the other direction he was startled to see some of the Chizman warriors returning.

Stumbling to his feet, he ran after Naomi and the plump professor. "Come on!" he grunted urgently. "They're all coming back! Make for the place where those flashes came from!"

Cochran grunted something unintelligible.

"What were they?" asked Naomi.

"Haven't a clue," snapped Brandon, glancing over his shoulder. Torches were waving towards the lion pit now. He hoped they could escape in the prevailing darkness, but it would be a close thing if they did succeed.

The gloom of the trees swallowed them up and gave them much-needed shelter. But the voice of a Chizman was lifted loudly as the man set off in pursuit after finding the unconscious body of the high priest.

"I can't run much further!" gasped Cochran thickly. "You two go on. I'll be all right!"

"Keep going!" snapped Brandon tersely. "We're not going to leave anyone behind!"

They blundered on.

Then dark figures rose in their path, blocking their way.

Brandon stiffened and halted in his tracks. He saw three shapeless forms in front of him. Clenching his fists he started forward again, determined to break through if it was the last thing he ever did.

"Hey, take it easy, will you?' said a voice as he began to strike out in the darkness.

Brandon froze, too staggered to believe the evidence of his own cars. He knew that voice, and the whole thing was far too incredible to register on his faculties after the strain of the last long minutes.

Cochran gasped something under his breath. Then the voice of Naomi broke through the momentary silence.

"Jeff! Jeff, is that really you?"

"Have to be a ghost if it wasn't!" came Lambert's curt words. "Come on, you lot, we're on our way!"

Brandon sighed deeply. He could still not believe it, but it seemed to be true. Maybe this was the strange explanation of the flashes and balls of fire that had turned defeat to victory and saved him and Cochran from the pit of lions. He could not even guess at the methods Lambert had used, nor could he understand how the young man was still alive, but it was now established fact.

Suddenly someone else was beside him, grasping his arm firmly and helping him along as he stumbled forward in the wake of Lambert and Naomi.

Peering through the deep darkness of the tree-covered jungle, he saw that his companion was a grinning N'gambi. A yard or so away was the little native girl, Tsakim, She had attached herself to Professor Cochran, acting as his guide in their hurried retreat from the vicinity of the Pit of Lions.

"N'gambi," muttered Brandon in a stupefied manner. "I thought I'd seen the last of you. By God, it's good to know you're alive! How did you manage it?"

"*Bwana,*" whispered N'gambi, "it was not I who did this thing, but the white man, Lambert. He came from the night and killed the guard who stood to watch us. Then he uses strange weapons and sends up fire into the sky. Tsakim and I were afraid, but we knew he was a good man and not an enemy. And he had a bow and arrow stolen from the dead guard. It was good that I could use it well, for I killed the lion by creeping through the trees and shooting it."

Brandon grinned at N'gambi's description. "You certainly worked a fast one there," he said as they ran on.

Not for some time did they have another chance to talk.

With Lambert in the lead and Naomi at his side, the little party of fugitives thrust their way through the jungle in the general direction of the side of the vast well.

By this time Brandon had lost all sense of location. He was merely moving blindly along in the wake of the others, not caring where he went so long as he got some rest before many hours passed.

N'gambi stuck close to his employer, while up in front Jeff Lambert was leading the white girl to safety.

Then Cochran said: "Where are we heading, Jeff?"

"Somewhere where we can climb out of this hole," answered Lambert.

Brandon was trying to follow the conversation now, but his head was buzzing and his legs felt on the point of giving way. Had it not been for N'gambi he would have fallen a dozen times.

It was then that the sound of the long-drawn, warning call of the distant silver horn was heard.

"That means they're going to use the gorillas again," muttered Cochran. "I do hate those things!"

"They hate us, too," grunted Lambert. "Let's hold up a moment and get our bearings. I'm not far off being lost myself just now."

They paused in their headlong flight, panting for breath. Brandon sank to the ground, closing his eyes. N'gambi said: "The *Bwana* Brandon is wounded. He should be looked at."

Cochran knelt beside him, examining the torn and bleeding flesh where the lion's claws had struck him down during the fight in the pit. They gathered round Brandon anxiously. He managed to grin up at them then.

"Don't worry about me," he said grimly. "I'm fine; but I could do with a drink if anyone's got such a thing."

Lambert immediately brought out a small flask from his bush shirt pocket and un-stoppered it quickly.

"Here," he said. "Take a pull from that."

"Where are we?" queried Cochran in some bewilderment.

They all listened, their heads on one side, straining their ears for a sound of danger if it happened to be close.

From not such a long way off came the sound of falling water.

"That's the waterfall!" exclaimed Cochran elatedly. "If we can reach it we can rest up for a while and get our strength back before we make a break."

"Not a bad idea," agreed Lambert. "I thought I knew quite a bit about this well, but you've got something there."

Brandon, stronger from his brief respite, walked forward with Lambert now. He was puzzled by a lot of things, and wondered if they could clear them up while they had the chance.

"I thought you were dead," he began.

"Can't kill me!" grinned Lambert. "That buffalo had a darned good try, but he only knocked me for six over the edge of the well."

"You must have landed lightly," commented Brandon.

"In a tree half way down the drop. It saved me and knocked me unconscious at the same time. By the time I came round there was no sign of you so I climbed down and was roaming around the well on my own."

"Pity we couldn't have joined forces," said Brandon.

Lambert chuckled. "Easier said than done," he replied. "As a matter of fact I saw you several times. I wasn't far off when the Chizmans captured you and the professor, but I daren't let you know."

"Hmmm..." grunted Brandon. He decided that Lambert was a remarkably lucky person one way and another. Then:

"Now let us into the secret of how you pulled off that firework show a while ago," he said. "I'm just about dying of curiosity."

They hurried on through the scrub for several minutes before Lambert answered. By now they were nearing the waterfall and the cave behind it.

Suddenly N'gambi, a little in front, stopped abruptly, turning to the others with upraised hand.

The crash of swift movement reached their ears. Some large creature was coming towards them through the undergrowth. Lambert pulled a Verey pistol from his pocket. "Balls of fire!" he muttered. "One cartridge left!"

12

THE CAVE

IN THE faint luminosity that seeped down through the foliage, Brandon caught sight of the Verey pistol and understood some of the previous happenings, though how Lambert had come to find such an unorthodox weapon was beyond him.

However, there was no time for speculation.

The six fugitives huddled together, peering through the gloom in an effort to discover what manner of threat they were up against.

Then to their dismay they heard the sound of the warning horn not twenty yards distant.

"My God, they've outflanked us!" muttered Lambert grimly. "Now what do we do?" He gripped the big Verey pistol tightly, but as yet there was no target at which to shoot.

N'gambi, armed with the looted bow and arrow, stood ready for action. Tsakim stood close at his side, while Cochran and Brandon were rigid in their tracks, listening with bated breath.

They heard further noises, all of them closer than before.

"Coming in a line," whispered Brandon. "Sweeping across the entire place by the sound of it. We'd better move."

"Maybe you're right," came the answer.

Cochran crept towards them. "If we can reach the cave we'll be safe for a time," he breathed. "Follow me!"

Brandon nodded. "That's our best bet," he answered.

They started moving forward again with the greatest caution. Away to left and right, almost level with them, were noises of stealthy advance. Then came the sound of the horn again. It echoed eerily through the trees and undergrowth as they elbowed their way ahead.

The waterfall was close now. Its tumbling music nearly drowned the crashing, creaking sound of the gorilla cohorts as they combed the jungle.

No word was spoken between the fugitives. They felt themselves being hunted like wild animals, relying on their own silence and stealth to escape from death. It was nerve-wracking work, and Brandon's weakened condition did nothing to improve it. Even a man as powerful and fearless as Brandon could not hope to fight a couple of lions and get away unscathed. He knew he was lucky to have escaped with his life.

But that was over and done with. They were now in danger from other sources, and those sources might strike at any moment.

Limping painfully through the bush, Brandon found his thoughts reverting to all manner of unexpected incidents that had taken place during the time he had been in the well. But he thrust them from his mind with a firm resolution. His head was swimming and he had an idea that although he was on his feet he would not remain standing if he allowed his mind to drift. In fact, he recognised his condition as being so close to collapse as to make no matter. If he stopped again he would not go on. The thought was a sobering one.

"Hurry!" urged Cochran tightly. "Not far to go now."

Heard distinctly against the background of the waterfall, came the noises of the advancing, searching gorillas and their Chizman attendants.

Lambert, his face drawn with worry, glanced round with anxious eyes.

"I don't like it," he whispered to Brandon. "They seem to be in front of us as, well as alongside. If you ask me we're more or less surrounded."

"I'm not asking anyone." jerked Brandon wearily. "Just keep going or we shan't even make the cave."

"Will it save us when we do?" queried Naomi doubtfully. "I'm completely lost, so don't count on me as much help."

"You've been grand, kid," whispered Lambert, gripping her arm firmly. They hurried on, not daring to relax their vigilance or slow their advance.

Again came the rallying call of the silver horn. This time it was so close that the native girl almost cried aloud.

"Seems they have our destination taped already," muttered Cochran. There was a hint of panic and desperation in his voice.

"Don't give up hope," said Lambert softly. "We're almost there now."

It was true; the glimmer of falling water was plain to see in front of them. It fell from high above in a long silver curtain of spray, dampening the night air and making it cool where before it had been almost suffocating. Brandon felt the coolness as a wonderful relief on his flushed and torn face.

They stumbled on, their feet slow and heavy now after the strain of flight. And all around them was the movement of the searching gorillas.

Suddenly, when they were less than a dozen yards from the edge of the waterfall and the stream that carried it away, Lambert, leading with his Verey pistol, halted abruptly, bringing up his weapon and pointing it forwards.

Looming large in their path, was a wild-looking monster gorilla. It caught sight of the human beings at the same time as Lambert spotted it. The animal gave a snarling, grunting roar. Then its bellow of challenge rolled out through the night, a frightening sound. The creature stood there, roaring and beating at its chest with enormous clenched fists.

"That'll bring 'em running!" snapped Brandon harshly.

Answering cries and the music of the horn rang out in the surrounding gloom. The crashing of broken foliage was loud on all sides.

"We've got to get through!" snapped Lambert curtly.

As he spoke he levelled his pistol. There was a dull bang as he fired; then a brilliant ball of orange-coloured fire shot out towards the savage sentinel that barred their path.

The gorilla gave a terrified roar as it saw the ball of fire shooting towards it. It ducked involuntarily and tried to escape, but Lambert's aim had been good. The burning ball of flame smacked the creature full in the chest, making it scream out in agony and anger. It was bowled over by the shock, but it could not shake off the burning globe that was killing it.

The ball of fire was deeply imbedded in its hairy flesh.

Rolling and screaming on the ground, it gave the fugitive party a chance to escape. Led by Lambert, now brandishing the empty and useless Verey pistol, they darted forward, past the writhing animal in the direction of the waterfall.

But by this time other gorillas and their Chizman guards were closing in. Brandon caught sight of another monster bearing down on their right flank. He yelled a warning to N'gambi, who stopped instantly and drew back his bow. There was a twang as the shaft left the bow, then it was quivering in the gorilla's heart as the creature tried vainly to pluck it out. A moment later it pitched over, dead.

"Nice work!" snapped Brandon. "Run for the waterfall! They're coming at us!"

Several of the animals and savage Chizmans were now in view, dark shapes in the gloom. But the way to the edge of the tumbling water was clear—for a moment or two more.

With a rush the party gained their objective. Lambert hesitated, not sure of how the land lay. Instantly the professor dived into the lead. The rest followed close on his heels. N'gambi, carrying their only weapon, brought up the rear, pausing in front of the cave entrance for just long enough to send an arrow into the stomach of the nearest of the Chizman warriors. Then he was bending double and ducking under the water and seeking the blackness behind it where his leaders waited.

Angry snarls greeted their disappearance, for the men as well as the gorillas felt themselves cheated of their prey. Now Cochran turned and sank to the ground in the utter darkness of the cave. Brandon, too, found that his legs would no longer support him. Lambert and the others were in better shape, though the girls were feeling the strain of flight more than they cared to admit.

It was Lambert who felt in his pocket and produced a cigarette lighter. The flame it gave was infinitely small in comparison with the enormity of the darkness, but at least it gave them some inkling of what their immediate surroundings were like.

"Hmmmph!" Professor Cochran peered round intently. "First time I've seen the inside of this place," he said. "Used it as a hideout when I got away from the devils, but I didn't have a light in those days!"

N'gambi turned his head and grinned broadly. He was stationed close to the entrance of the cave, peering out into the water-shielded night, his bow and arrow half drawn back in readiness to meet the next move on the part of the enemy.

Lambert settled Naomi down out of harm's way. When he came across to Brandon his face was worried and drawn in the flickering flame of the cigarette lighter.

"What's worrying you?" asked Brandon wearily.

"I should say we were trapped!" grunted Lambert uneasily. "They aren't likely to let us walk out of here alive, are they? That stands to reason!" He held his lighter up high and stared round grimly. The six of them were close together in the darkness, for there was little enough room in any event. Four or five yards out was the entrance of the cave, screened off by the falling water, with barely a couple of feet between its fall and the cave mouth.

N'gambi bent forward suddenly as Brandon looked round.

"Something is happening, *bwana*," he said over his shoulder. "They are going to come in after us."

"Hold 'em as long as you can!" snapped Brandon. The weariness seemed to drop from his body like a cloak. He came up behind N'gambi, peering over his shoulder with narrowed eyes, straining to see through the darkness and the curtain of protective spray that screened the entrance.

Beyond the rush and roar of the water he thought he could hear the shouting of men and the bellow of the gorillas. It was an unpleasant sensation to realise that their enemies had them cornered; worse still to think that they had put themselves in this unenviable position. They had no one to blame for seeking the shelter of the cave. It had been a natural choice under the circumstances. Now it looked as if it would be the end of them.

Without any warning a large and shapeless mass burst through and was silhouetted against the faintly luminous fall of water.

Without a word N'gambi drew his bow and sent an arrow straight out at the shape.

Even against the sound of the waterfall they could all hear the bellow of pain that greeted the shot. But N'gambi was not easy in his mind. He had driven off the beast sent in by the Chizmans, but there were only two arrows left in the leather quiver slung from his broad back. One wasted might mean their lives.

Brandon did not need to be told what worried his headman. He used his eyes and saw the reason himself, but said nothing.

"Any chance of getting out?" queried Lambert. He had just extinguished his cigarette lighter on the advice of the Professor.

"Save it till we need it more urgently, son," Cochran had said. "They don't burn for long, those darned things. Most times they won't even light when you want 'em!"

Brandon said: "Stay there, N'gambi. Don't use those arrows unless you have to. I'll be back in a moment." He turned, gripping Cochran's arm tightly. "You know this cave, Professor," he said quietly, his voice just audible above the sound of rushing water. "Didn't you feel you way around it when you came in first?"

"Not a lot," answered Cochran in some surprise "Why?"

"I've got an idea," said Brandon. "When the light was on a moment ago I thought I saw an opening in the back wall. Let's take a look."

"Jeff!" called Cochran. "Let's have some light, son! There may be another way out of this dump."

Lambert immediately flicked his lighter into flame.

Brandon took it carefully in his hand and moved as far to the back of the shallow cave as he could. What he saw there confirmed his earlier hopes. Low down near the floor was a hole large enough for a man to get through if he bent half double.

"Shall we try it?" he said. "It's a chance in a million, but we can't ignore it. Before long they'll have us cold from outside. We might as well take a chance."

They looked at him in the faint light, nodding at the suggestion.

Cochran eyed the hole in the wall of the cave with a doubtful stare.

"All right," he said loudly. "It's O.K. by me, but how about the girls?"

Naomi glanced at Lambert. "Anywhere you say," she replied. "If we stay here we shall all be killed in the end—or die if they don't come in after us. We can't lose anything, can we?"

Tsakim came close to Brandon. "Where the *bwana* goes I will gladly follow," she murmured.

"Come on then!" said Brandon. His mouth was tight as he turned away and stepped towards the second entrance. For all he knew it might only be a false hope he had raised, but that was something he must chance.

Bending low, holding the lighter before him, he entered the hole in the wall, peering forward keenly. The flame of the lighter was reflected dully by close rock walls. The air smelt stale and heavy. It was not a good sign, he thought grimly.

"Stay close," he threw over his shoulder. "There's a tunnel of sorts, but it may be a dead end." Then he was stooping along, working deeper and deeper into the tunnel.

To his surprise it sloped upwards sharply after a few yards. He wondered desperately if it actually communicated with the upper ground.

The others were following him. N'gambi came right behind him, still with the bow and arrow. Then came the Professor, puffing and blowing like a grampus. Tsakim and Naomi came next, with Jeff Lambert bringing up the rear.

The further they went the more distant was the muffled roar of the waterfall.

Brandon, feeling fatigue spreading over him again, came to a halt. He found that he could now stand upright, for the roof of the tunnel had lifted considerably since they entered it. He leant against the wall, breathing deeply. The wounds on his chest and arms were stinging and giving him pain. Some of them, stiffened by the air, had broken open again and were bleeding freely. Some had never stopped bleeding, though not in a way that was serious. But he recognised the fact that he was weak and had lost a lot of blood.

Then Lambert's voice reached him from the rear. There was only room for one man at a time in the width of the tunnel.

"What is it?" called Brandon. His tone was edged with weariness; but there was a sense of partial triumph inside him now. "What is it?" he repeated. "I can't hear."

"Someone or something is coming up behind us!" called back Lambert.

"All right," Brandon answered. "N'gambi, get back there with the bow. Come on, the rest of you."

He forced himself onwards, climbing steadily now with the rising floor of the tunnel. He seemed to have be climbing for hours, so heavy did his limbs feel.

A yell from behind brought his head round; but there was a note in the yell that held triumph. It was N'gambi. He had been forced to use one of the precious arrows. Naomi shouted the news to Brandon. N'gambi had killed one of the Chizmans who had penetrated the tunnel in their rear.

Brandon pressed on. Word was passed up to him that more of the enemy were coming up behind. He barely heeded the warning, for he saw that the walls of the tunnel were closing in again, leaving hardly room for him to move. He had to stoop right down, even crawling at one point, so low did the roof come.

"There's one thing," he shot back to his friends: "they won't get the gorillas on our tail!"

"If it gets much smaller you'll be leaving me stuck in it for good!" grunted Cochran. "I carry more weight than you do, Brandon!"

Brandon grinned humourlessly. Then, when he thought the tunnel was getting even narrower, he saw something ahead that made his pulses race.

Halting once more, panting and sweating from the exertion of the laborious climb, he stared forwards. The flame of the cigarette lighter flickered dangerously in a faint waft of breeze.

"What's the matter?" demanded someone behind him.

"I can see the sky," he said quietly, almost reverently.

"Thank God!" whispered Naomi.

"Men come behind us, *bwana,*" said N'gambi. "It is well that we do not stay for long."

"Just getting my breath," he grunted. "Come on!"

The faintly brighter patch of star-lit sky was visible through a hole at the end of the tunnel. To Brandon it seemed a very long way off, though he knew it could not be more than fifteen yards or so distant. He crawled on. N'gambi in the rear, though he could not see a thing in the darkness, reported someone else close behind them.

Brandon was on the point of telling him to use the bow and the last of the arrows when the words froze on his lips.

Blocking out the tiny patch of sky was a moving shape. He halted and stared at it aghast. Then the gleam of the lighter flame was reflected back at him in two glowing green sparks of wicked light. All the vindictiveness of the wild was condensed in the pair of eyes that watched him from the darkness ahead. They were eyes that chilled his blood as he met

Jungle Allies

their cold hard stare.

Then the eyes were coming closer as the creature moved.

Brandon gulped. "Save that arrow, N'gambi!" he said. "Pass it up to me, quickly!"

The arrow reached him. There was no room to use the bow, for the tunnel was narrowing. Brandon must face the savage animal in front with a wooden arrow as his only weapon.

He went forward slowly, in darkness now. Then the hot breath of the wild beast was warming his face. He could hear it just ahead. Even as he paused it sprang. He held the arrow rigidly, straight out in front of him. There was a terrific impact that shook his whole body, then he felt his arms being slashed afresh by razor sharp claws. He had no strength left to resist or fight back, but by the luck of the very devil the wooden arrow had penetrated the animal's throat. It had killed itself, in fact, and was impaled on the arrow, still alive, but finished.

They backed down out of range of its death throes. When Brandon, right at the end of his tether, lit the lighter again, they saw the body of a full-grown leopard. Getting past it and out of the tunnel was quite a job, but in the end they managed it.

Escape came shortly before the dawn. They found that the tunnel came up among the ruined masonry they had stumbled on in the jungle not far from the edge of the well where the People of the Sun lived. But their enemies were not done yet. A tall Chizman wormed his way of the tunnel close behind them, to be met by Lambert with a chunk of rock. Beaten on the head, the Chizman, brave though he was, perished in a moment.

"Close the tunnel!" shouted Cochran. He grab some of the fallen boulders of the ruined masonry, piling them into the mouth of the tunnel, filling it up. The others joined him. Any hope the Chizmans might have had of reaching them was now gone.

A few minutes later the party struck off through the jungle, slowly and painfully, but triumphantly for all that. Brandon was tended by Tsakim, who bathed his wounds. Naomi and Lambert seemed to have a great deal to say in very quiet voices. Professor Cochran was busy rambling on about the wonderful race of lost people they had been among.

"Fine!" said Brandon, grinning. "They're wonderful, but not so hot when they capture you! Bear that in mind if you're thinking of coming this way again!"

N'gambi smiled knowingly. He and Tsakim were together when the girl was not nursing Brandon—which he didn't allow for long. There had been no sign of pursuit from the People of the Sun, but they covered as much ground as they could while the going was good.

Not until three or four days later did Brandon learn how Lambert had worked his firework display.

Questioned, Lambert grinned. "Well," he said. "I was wandering around when I came on a lot of the photographic equipment from the Professor's expedition. The Chizmans must have dumped it when they didn't understand it. I was lucky. There were a few flash-bulbs and a battery there. I used them, as well as the Verey pistol which was also with the rest of the gear. That's all there was to it, but it worked wonders as far as we were concerned."

"It certainly did," agreed Brandon. "There were odd moments when I didn't think we'd get out of that place, you know?"

Lambert chuckled and slid an arm round Naomi's waist.

"You don't say!" he said. "Funny, but I had the same sort of feeling more than once myself! If you had the chance would you visit the people of Chizma again, Rex?"

Brandon considered for a moment. "That would depend," he said thoughtfully. "Yes, it would depend on a lot of things." He felt in the pocket of his tattered bush shirt. When his hand came out again it was clenched on something. He looked at Naomi and Jeff, eyes twinkling. "I think," he said, "that you two will have more use for this than I shall. Keep it. Keep it as a souvenir of the time when the Chizmans made you a goddess, Naomi. Here, take it."

He opened his fingers as the girl stared at him in wonderment. In the palm of his hand lay the glittering diamond presented to him by the pygmy chief. It was a fitting gift for Naomi Jensen, Goddess of the People the Sun.

THE END

DENIS HUGHES

Denis (Talbot) Hughes (1917-2008)

Born in London, England, Hughes was the son of noted Victorian artist Talbot Hughes. He was training as a pilot during WW2, when a serious crash ended his flying career. Attracted to writing by the expanding post-war market in paperback publishing, his first book (an espionage thriller) was published in 1948.

Over the next six years, an astonishing more than 80 novels followed, chiefly westerns and science fiction, with a dozen jungle-adventure novels.

In 1950, his UK publisher Curtis Warren had launched their six-novel *Azan the Apeman* series, written by "Marco Garron" (David Griffiths), commissioned after the hugely successful Mark Goulden/W. H. Allen (later Pinnacle Books) reprints of ERB's Tarzan novels.

But the 'Azan the Apeman' banner was such a blatant copy of Tarzan that E.R.B. Inc. threatened Curtis with prosecution unless the books were taken off the market.

To cover their losses, in May 1951 Curtis Warren brought Denis Hughes into the writing seat and a new series of jungle adventures began, this time featuring his original character, Rex Brandon. To capitalize on their earlier series, Curtis Warren issued the books under the byline of

'Marco Garon' (only one 'r' in 'Garon').

These fast-moving action-packed novels books were successful enough for the publisher and author to issue a further six titles in 1951, and another four in 1952. Most of these short novels have decidedly fantastic elements, and are infused with the same weird imagination Hughes displayed in his many 'science fantasy' novels. All of them are set in the African jungle, except for the last one, Mountain Gold, which, exceptionally, is a 'straight' adventure set in the Yukon.

When his main publisher collapsed in 1954, Hughes switched to writing exclusively for the established D.C. Thomson, famous publisher of boys' papers. Until his retirement in the 1980s Hughes became one of their mainstay (albeit anonymous) writers for such comics as Victor, Hotspur, Wizard and Warlord (the latter title inspired by Hughes' "Scarlet Pimpernel" type WW2 secret agent character, Lord Peter Flint, alias 'Warlord'.)

Because most of his novels had been published pseudonymously, Hughes fell out of print for many years, until researcher Philip Harbottle revealed his authorship. Since then all of his 'lost' novels are currently being reprinted under his real name.

WATCH FOR MORE ADVENTURES OF
REX BRANDON
JUNGLE HUNTER

1 | THE ADVENTURES OF REX BRANDON, JUNGLE HUNTER BY DENIS HUGHES
DEATH WARRIORS
REX BRANDON
JUNGLE HUNTER

3 | THE ADVENTURES OF REX BRANDON, JUNGLE HUNTER BY DENIS HUGHES
BLACK FURY
REX BRANDON
JUNGLE HUNTER

Coming soon from
WWW.BOLDVENTUREPRESS.COM

REX BRANDON: JUNGLE HUNTER TM & © 2023 The Estate of Denis Hughes. Used with permission.

An iron-fisted ex-Confederate sergeant ...
A gun-slinging ex-Union captain...
Destiny paired them to hunt for a fortune in gold ...
To pursue the thief ... To brave a thousand perils!

BENEDICT™
AND BRAZOS

by E. JEFFERSON CLAY

*"**Aces Wild** [#1] is a really entertaining traditional Western with a pair of likable protagonists ... I'll be reading more of them, you can count on that. Recommended."*

James Reasoner, *Rough Edges*

WWW.BOLDVENTUREPRESS.COM

Benedict And Brazos
TM & © 2023
Piccadilly Publishing.
All Rights Reserved.

ABRAHAM STROUD

Inventor, scientist, CEO
Vampire hunter ...
He knew the job was dangerous ...

BLOODSCREAMS™

by ROBERT W. WALKER

A cross between Nikola Tesla and T.E. Lawrence; A direct descendant of Abraham Van Helsing, maintaining the family business — *hunting vampires and supernatural vermin*. Follow along in his amazing adventures ... if you dare ...

Bloodscreams TM & © 2023 Robert W. Walker. All rights reserved.

Printed in Great Britain
by Amazon